MEN in UNIFORM

Courteous, courageous and commanding—
these heroes lay it all on the line for the
people they love in more than fifty stories about
loyalty, bravery and romance.
Don't miss a single one!

TORI
CARRINGTON

THE WOMAN FOR
DUSTY CONRAD

Published by Silhouette Books

America's Publisher of Contemporary Romance

 SILHOUETTE BOOKS

Recycling programs for this product may not exist in your area.

ISBN-13: 978-0-373-36270-7

THE WOMAN FOR DUSTY CONRAD

TORI CARRINGTON

Bestselling authors Lori and Tony Karayianni are the husband-and-wife team behind the pen name Tori Carrington, and are the winners of an *RT Book Reviews* Career Achievement Award for Series Fiction. Their August 2009 Harlequin Blaze novel, *Unbridled,* marked their forty-fifth published title...and they have no plans to slow down anytime soon. For more info on the couple and their titles, and to enter their monthly online drawings, visit them at www.toricarrington.net.

In loving memory of Kostoula Karayianni,
who dedicated more than twenty-five years to the
Athens Fire Department, and her entire life to her family.
You are deeply missed.

Chapter 1

Dusty Conrad's mission was simple. Go into the firehouse. Seek out Jolie. Get her to sign the divorce papers she'd had for two months. Move on with his life. Let Jolie get on with hers.

Simple. *Right.* Then why was he driving around the narrow, tree-lined streets of Old Orchard, going everywhere but the fire station?

Dusty tightened his hands on the steering wheel of the shiny red pickup and visually inhaled his surroundings. He took in the hay bundles decorated with pumpkins, the witch and black-cat decals clinging to the windows of the older homes that lined Main Street, the colorful mums dotting nearly every free space. Funny. Only six months had passed since he'd left. Somehow it seemed just like yesterday. Except that now the town had on its Halloween best, ready to partake in the spooky festivities unquestionably scheduled for the weekend. Six months ago budding tree branches had borne pastel eggs and windows had sported cute caricatures of rabbits and baskets.

Bustling was one word he'd never use to describe the Rockwellesque streets of Old Orchard, Ohio. No. Rather the word *sluggish* came to mind as he left the residential section of Main and slowly drove into the quaint downtown area. As he veered to the right to navigate around Lucas Circle, he watched young Dana Malone as she tried to teach her son Josh how to look both ways before crossing the street. The toddler, however, seemed to have other ideas, like trying to climb into the gargantuan water fountain that had been designed some hundred and twenty years ago. The entire town had been built around Lucas Circle. It was where all town functions began and ended, the town meeting spot for union support rallies and carnivals alike. Just like the old, hulking cement structure of Old Jake's, a general store where everyone still shopped, despite the spreading cancer of strip malls a mere five-minute drive away.

He supposed the word *town* no longer fit the growing city now estimated at forty-five thousand. But while the modern semi-new hospital on the opposite end of Main Street and several towering office buildings had altered the skyline a bit, the heart of downtown looked pretty much as it had a century earlier. Three-

and four-story brick buildings crouched side by side for blocks on either side of Main Street and Old Orchard Avenue, storefronts holding advertisements for seven dollar haircuts, sporting neon beer signs and announcing daily specials. With the majestic trees, the old stone library and the turn-of-the-century church, the small-town flavor remained. An essence carefully and lovingly tended to by Old Orchard's citizens, the majority of whom still chose to walk instead of drive, frequented the smaller shops rather than heading out to the cheaper strip malls and large chain stores nearby, and were never too busy to say hello and stop for a brief chat, or help out a neighbor in need. It was a place where if you didn't directly know a person, you knew someone who did. Some might find conversations dotted with "you know, Jim Olsen's cousin's husband's aunt" difficult to follow, but here such connections were the norm.

Dusty finished negotiating Lucas Circle and absently rubbed at a spot just below his rib cage, at the needling ache there. Old Orchard was where he'd been born. Where he'd passed every major milestone, from first step, to first sexual experience. He knew just where to look for items in Old Jake's General Store on the corner, be it his favorite candy bar or condoms. Knew that the unseasonable warmth of the late October day would glide into a crisp autumn night. Could remember that if you hit the curb just right with the front tire of your bicycle, you could either pop an awesome wheelie…or lose your front teeth. He could practically hear the old church bell missing a ring as it chimed off the time, and the sound

of the kids being let out of school on the outskirts of town
and the hum of lawnmowers as homeowners saw to the
last of the garden chores before winter set in.

He could also practically hear the echo of his younger
brother Erick's mischievous laughter riding on the
gentle breeze and smell Jolie's subtle perfume entwined
with the scent of autumn leaves.

Once outside Lucas Circle he continued down Main
and reluctantly picked up speed, reaching his destination quicker than he intended. He slowly pulled to a stop
outside Fire Station 2, then glanced at the building. The
renovated old schoolhouse looked exactly the same.
The tower clock was stuck at the same time—nine-
fifteen, the same moment it stopped back on June 6,
1982, when a fire had claimed the lives of two firefighters at the automobile-parts manufacturing plant five
miles outside town—and the white trim contrasted
neatly against the warm red brick. Then again, he hadn't
expected it to change any. He was the one who had
changed. So much he barely recognized the man who
had spent nearly as much time running to the station
than from it, perpetually late. Even now he fought the
urge to glance at his watch to see that he was on time,
though no one would be clocking him in.

Two of the three bays were open to the midmorning
sun, revealing that one of the hulking red engines—the
hose truck—was missing, while the pumper stood
gleaming like a chrome-toothed animal.

"I'll be damned. Is that Dusty Conrad?" a familiar
voice echoed from within the depths of the station.

Dusty watched his old friend John Sparks step out

from the side of the remaining engine, wiping his hands on a soft leather cloth, a mile-wide grin on his too-handsome face. He wore his gray-and-black sheriff's uniform, telling Dusty that his penchant for hanging around the fire station hadn't changed any. And seeing as Sparks had started out at the fire station, no one complained about his being there. Especially since he enjoyed helping out.

Dusty began to step toward the open bay when another man stepped from the shadows behind John. The pinprick in his chest turned into a tangible pain as he realized he'd half expected to see his brother, Erick, stepping out after John. But no matter how similar in build and coloring the unfamiliar man—more kid—with Sparks was, he could never be Erick. His brother was gone. And Dusty was the one to blame.

Realization seemed to spread across Sparks's face. He looked down, then hooked a thumb in the kid's direction. "This is Scott Wahl. You remember him, don't you? Think a foot or two shorter—"

"Scooter." Dusty nodded, finally recognizing the blond-haired teen. Whenever the station team conducted school classes and drills, or demonstrations at the county fair, Scott, aka Scooter, had always been the one to dog them every step of the way. He must have graduated to actually hanging out at the station.

Growing aware of the uncomfortable silence, he switched his gaze to John Sparks. The shorter, wiry man had been Erick's best friend. All throughout elementary, middle and high school nothing had been able to separate the two.

Nothing but death.

"Hey, Sparks, how have you been?" he asked, finding it difficult to face the only person on earth who had been as close to his brother as he.

John's ready grin always caught him off guard. As did his strength when he came out and shook Dusty's hand so vigorously he might have vibrated him straight out of his work boots before giving him a brief, awkward "guy" kind of half hug. "I'd say you were a sight for sore eyes, Conrad, but with you looking like a paint can just fell on your head, I can't."

Dusty lifted his free hand to his light brown hair. "Funny you should say that. A paint can did fall on me. Two days ago on a work site."

John's grin never budged. "It was rumored you were working in construction in Toledo."

"Yeah. Nothing much ever escaped town gossip, did it? Sneeze and those on the outskirts called to bless you."

"That's Old Orchard, all right." John slapped a hand across his shoulders and they walked toward the open bay door. "You back for good?"

Back for good? Dusty slowed his step, an odd foreboding taking root in his stomach. He glanced at his friend and absently rubbed the back of his neck. When he'd left, he'd done so without any intention of returning. John's sincere expression told him he expected otherwise.

"Nope," he finally said in answer. "Just back for a visit."

When he'd left, he'd done so without talking to anyone but Jolie. He'd never stopped to consider how she might explain his absence. Even if he had, he would have guessed she'd put it as simply as possible. Say something along the lines that after the death of his brother, he'd lost his nerve…both as a firefighter and her husband.

He would never have thought that she might not explain it at all.

A full minute passed before Dusty's eyesight adjusted from the bright sunlight to the dimness of the station as they stepped into the open bay. "Jolie around?" he asked as casually as he could, though just forming his mouth around her name did something funny to his stomach.

John shook his head. "She, Martinez and Sal are out on a run."

Dusty wasn't surprised. If a truck was gone, then Jolie was on it. "Nothing serious, I hope."

John chuckled. "Not unless you're a chicken farmer. One of Rudy Glick's chicken trucks overturned over on Route 108 with a full load. Yeah, I'd say Jolie and the guys have their hands pretty full right about now."

At the sound of their voices, the remaining members of Group 1, the team scheduled for duty that day, came out from the back room. Dusty weathered a swarm of back pats, arm slugs and hearty greetings from the men he'd spent a good chunk of his life with fighting fires.

"There is a God," Gary Jones, the chief, moaned, his gray hair tucked under a station ball cap. "I haven't had a decent meal around here since the day you left, Dusty."

Sparks patted Gary's round middle. "Not that you could tell."

"Watch it, boy, or I'll ban you from the station." A grin smoothed the edge off his words. "Either that or retire now instead of in a few weeks, leaving the town in the lurch. Then where would you be, Sheriff Sparks?"

"Ouch."

Dusty slid his fingers into his front jeans pockets. "Who's on kitchen detail now?"

"Martinez."

He winced. "I'm guessing he got stuck with it because of lack of seniority rather than any real skills in the kitchen."

"Yeah, well, it's not his skills we're questioning. It's his choice of foods. Refried beans are not something you want churning in your stomach when you're called off on a run." The guys laughed. "Anyway, we did try to enlist somebody else…." Jones's words drifted off even as his blue eyes twinkled. "You should have seen Jolie's face when we suggested she take over, you know, thinking she may have picked up a thing or two from you along the way."

Dusty scratched his chin. "I can imagine. You all must have thought it was the Fourth of July what with all the fireworks that suggestion should have launched."

Gary grimaced as he burrowed his fingers under the front of his ball cap. "Got that right. We nearly had to get out the hose. That little gal of yours sure has a temper, all right."

All at once Gary seemed to realize what he'd said, as did everyone else in the firehouse, setting off an uncomfortable silence. Even Scooter Wahl, hanging out on the fringes, looked ill at ease.

Sparks cleared his throat. "So how long you in town for, buddy?"

"I don't know yet...."

The strident sound of an engine horn bellowed through the house. They all turned to find the missing members of the team pulling into the drive. Behind the cab, Jolie jumped off the step onto the pavement, her heavy gear slowing her not at all.

Dusty was rendered completely speechless. Fool that he was, he hadn't considered how he'd feel when he laid eyes on Jolie again. Hadn't even thought to remember that just looking at her made him wonder if he'd just swallowed a handful of sand. Hadn't anticipated his intense physical reaction to her, a need, really, that always seemed to be there, just below the surface of his skin. Even in her turnout clothes, the bulky yellow fireproof and waterproof jacket and pants, she drew his gaze like a spotlight. The bright morning sun ignited the auburn strands in her hair, her cheeks were full of color, the adrenaline inspired by any run fairly emanating from her like a heady perfume.

Then she spotted him. Her blue eyes widened to the size of baseballs, then brightened with a happiness that sent Dusty's stomach careering down to land somewhere around the vicinity of his knees.

Simple. *Right.*

Dusty had the sinking sensation that nothing about this visit was going to be simple.

Joy surged through Jolie Calbert Conrad's veins sure and strong as she stared into the face of the man it seemed she had loved her entire life. How many times in the past few months had she imagined returning to the station to find Dusty there? No fewer than a dozen at least. But he never had been. Until now. And despite the weightless sensation in her stomach, her shallow breathing, and the heat that immediately rushed to her cheeks, she wasn't altogether sure how she felt about him being there now.

Especially since his coming here to the station, rather than stopping by the house, *their* house, didn't bode well for what he was doing back.

"Did you get those dangerous, rampaging chickens picked up?" the chief asked as Martinez climbed from behind the driver's seat.

"Dirty job, but somebody's gotta do it," he said. "The town is safe for all to walk the streets again."

"Hey, it's Dusty!" Martinez rushed her husband and gave him an awkward bear hug. Jolie envied him the simple gesture, if only for the physical contact it allowed. She averted her gaze, trying to push the desire to hug Dusty herself safely away.

She swallowed the sudden emotion clogging her throat. Hugging Dusty should be the last thing she wanted to do. After five years of marriage, and a whole lifetime together before that, six months had gone by with little word from him. Except, of course, those words that came through his attorney.

She shivered despite the sunshine warmth of the day and the heavy gear she wore.

Martinez made some comment on Dusty's getting a little soft around the middle, then said, "I can't tell you how glad I am to see you, buddy. Where in the hell have you been? How in the hell are you?"

"Fine," Dusty said, his gaze never leaving Jolie's face.

Suddenly Jolie's boots seemed made of cement rather than specially treated leather, and her gear weighed a ton. She felt as if she'd just come off from fighting a four-alarm fire rather than chasing chickens that had been granted unexpected clemency down the highway. Something brushed against her foot and she started, making her realize that while she may appear completely at ease at seeing her husband for the first time in six months, her nerves were pulled taut and her stomach burned so much it hurt. Almost as an after-thought, she looked down at the scrap of fur that wound itself around her ankles. The usually coolly indifferent station cat traced figure eights around her legs. Jolie grimaced as Spot nudged her with more power than she would have thought possible. She stumbled forward, then played it off as if she'd meant to do that. Plucking her hat from the truck cab, she began shrugging out of her coat. Spot followed.

"Dusty," she acknowledged, trying to treat him like any other fellow firefighter as she entered the station. Pretend she hadn't spent the first month after he'd left crying her way through the night, then the next month dreaming he'd come back.

But as she grew nearer to him, she became all too aware of how exactly he wasn't just a fellow firefighter. And it had more to do with just the plain gold band she still wore around her ring finger.

Dusty Conrad was her husband. The man who had promised to love and cherish and care for her until "death do us part." And though she hadn't checked with the pastor, she was sure that those vows in no way included a note that read, "Please forgive me," and a disappearing act that would have made Copperfield sit up and take notice.

Chief Jones cleared his throat. "Hey, Jolie, you schedule that annual physical yet?"

She glanced at Gary, as if unable to comprehend his words. "Not yet."

"You've only got till the end of the month, you know."

She nodded slowly. "I know." And to think, just this morning she was thinking how much she hated checking in for her annual physical. Compared to facing Dusty now, it came a distant second.

The brief exchange proved the silence-breaker and the guys started talking again, conversation centering on Dusty and his sudden return.

Jolie purposely jutted her chin out. No matter how good he looked standing there in those faded jeans and soft chambray shirt, she wasn't going to let on how loudly her hormones screamed or how much she wanted to pin him against the firehouse wall and make up for lost time. She wasn't about to reveal anything until she found out why he was here. And even then, it might not be a good idea to tell him how much she'd missed him.

"I'm going to clean up," she said to everybody and nobody in particular. She sprinted for the locker room, nearly tripping over the fluff of black-and-white fuzz that was Spot blocking her path. So much for making a graceful exit.

Well, hell, that hadn't gone quite as he'd expected.
Dusty cast a glance toward the empty kitchen

doorway and wondered exactly what Jolie had gone to clean up. He'd assumed she'd meant herself. But in the forty-five minutes since she'd been gone, she could have cleaned the showers, bunkhouse and both fire engines…with her toothbrush.

Anxious, he flipped over the chicken-fried steaks he was preparing, seeking comfort in his old familiar role as cook. But his mind wasn't having any of it. The truth was being here was a little too familiar. Too comfortable. And to think he'd purposely come to the station instead of going to the house because he'd been afraid of familiarity. Wanted to avoid the temptation of falling back into old routines.

If that was the case, then why was it taking every ounce of restraint he had to keep himself from going after Jolie in the back rooms? Not to confront her about their divorce papers, but to rediscover her mouth, relearn her taste, find out if the flame he'd glimpsed in her eyes a short while ago burned just as hot now as it had back when.

He cleared his throat, ordering his coiled muscles to relax, holding his long-denied libido in check.

He glanced behind him, although he knew exactly where each of his former fellow firefighters was sitting at the table without looking. As always, Jones was at the head of the table looking every bit like the chief, while Martinez leaned back, rocking the front legs of his chair from the floor, acting the renegade rookie ready to take on the world. John Sparks was smack-dab in the middle of everyone, his sheriff's shirt rolled up to his elbows, those same elbows resting against the tabletop, while Sal was snacking on something or other he'd pilfered from the refrigerator. Dusty fell right into the old routine of exchanging verbal jabs with them with far too much ease. Even found himself listening for the old bell alarm that would call them out on a run.

He glanced toward the doorway again, only this time Scott Wahl blocked his view. Dusty looked back to the cooktop, not wanting to compare how similar the young man was to his brother, Erick. Not wanting to think about the chair at the other end of the table that was left empty because Erick was no longer there to fill it.

"You were the cook?" Scooter asked, propping a too skinny hip against the counter next to the stove.

"Yeah." He tested the boiling potatoes with a fork.

"I always thought cooking was a sissy chore."

Dusty hiked a brow.

"Not to say that you're a sissy or anything," Scott said quickly, his spine snapping flagpole straight. "Actually the guys have been telling me how, you know, you are the best and everything—"

"Was," he absently corrected the boy. "I was the best." At least up until the point when he'd caused the death of his brother. "How old are you, Scooter?"

The kid looked relieved that he'd changed the subject. "Eighteen."

Eighteen. Dusty nearly burned himself on the skillet handle. Erick had been eighteen when he started hanging out at the fire station, not content to do other things until he turned twenty-one and qualified for being a firefighter. No, Erick had automatically expected an exception to be made for him. Of course, none was. But that hadn't stopped his younger brother from dogging their steps when they went out on runs. If not on his bike, then in his car.

"You eat, don't you?" he asked Scott.

"Yeah, of course I eat. If I didn't eat, I'd be dead."

Damn. "You trying to tell me you've lived eighteen years without preparing a single meal, Scooter?"

"Scott," the teenager said, the tips of his ears reddening. "Everyone calls me Scott now."

"Is that so?"

The boy nodded.

"All right, then, Scott it is. And you didn't answer my question."

The boy shrugged. "I've fixed stuff for myself. You know, like macaroni and cheese and frozen pizzas when my mom's not home. But that doesn't count."

"How so?"

Scott grinned. "Because no one but me eats it."

"Ah." He switched on the fire under the vegetables, then held out his fork. "Well, then, I think it's about time that changed."

The kid stared at the fork as though it was a wild hose he couldn't bring under control. Dusty chuckled. "Don't panic. Just keep an eye on those steaks. When they start to brown, they're done. Just take them out and put them on the plate over there."

"Mr. Conrad, I—"

Mr. Conrad? Dusty fought the urge to look around to see if his father had dropped in for a visit from Arizona. "It's Dusty, kid." He patted him so hard on the back, Scott nearly doubled over. "And I have complete faith in you."

"That's not what I'm worried about. I mean, I think it's cool and everything that you cook, but…I…"

"What? You never linked firefighting with cooking?" Dusty shook his head. "See, Scott, that's one of the things you have to learn around here if you hope to make a good…no, great firefighter. Every job, be it wiping down the engines, checking the gear, or cooking, is an important one. After all, where are the men going to get the energy to fight fires if they're not eating healthy food?"

Scott turned redder than the fire engine Dusty could see through the door. Behind them, the men snickered.

"We sure could use some of that money you're making in Toledo in the ante," Martinez said from the table, tapping the edge of his cards against the top. "That is, if you can handle the pressure."

Dusty grinned. There was no more than seventy-five cents on the table if there was a dollar. "Sorry, guys, but you're just going to have to squeak by without me. Bets are too rich for me."

He started for the door, giving up on restraint and intent on tracking Jolie down. He reached the doorway at the same time she popped into it from the other side. Her appearance should have eased the tension from Dusty's shoulders. Instead, seeing her pulled his muscles tighter.

It was the same reaction he'd always had when faced with Jolie. That stomach-tightening, breath-robbing, mouth-watering sensation that if he didn't kiss her within ten seconds he'd die. And six months away from her had only made the reaction more acute. Which definitely didn't bode well for his mission.

"Hey, hey, hey, there she is," Jones called out. "Now, here's somebody not afraid of losing a few dollars."

Dusty noted the way Jolie avoided eye contact with him. For all the attention she'd paid him since she'd returned from her run, he was beginning to feel as if he were invisible. A nonentity unworthy of her attention. Which was no less than he deserved, he supposed. If only her unexplained emotional distance hadn't been part of his reason for leaving in the first place.

He hadn't meant to make their…meeting again so public. He'd thought about showing up at the house without letting anyone else know he was in town, then realized that was wishful thinking. The moment his truck rolled over the county line half the population probably already knew he was back, and by the time he parked it, his return was probably old news.

Ah, hell, who was he kidding? He'd come to the station on purpose. Had needed to be surrounded by others in order to make what he had to say go down easier…both for him and her.

Jolie skirted the table. "Sorry, guys, I'm going to pass tonight."

Exaggerated groans followed her to the refrigerator, where she pulled out salad fixings, then dropped them to the counter next to the stove.

From next to Dusty came an audible swallow. He didn't kid himself into thinking Jolie had made the giveaway sound. No, Scooter looked like he'd rather be in the skillet with the steaks, rather than watching over them. "Um, Mr. Conrad. I mean Dusty…"

Now that Jolie was where he wanted her, at least for

the moment, Dusty accepted the fork from Scott and turned the steaks out onto the plate. "Your instincts were straight on, Scooter. Trust them."

"Okay."

The teenager too happily turned cooking duty back over to him, all but scuttling to the chair he'd abandoned at the table. The rest of the men gladly dealt him into their next hand of poker.

But now that Dusty had the opening he'd been looking for, all his rehearsed words drained from his brain like water through a sieve. Taking his cue from Scott, he cleared his throat and slanted a glance toward Jolie. With neat, violent strokes of a knife, she made quick work of the salad. He was afraid if he didn't say something now, she'd finish and likely up and disappear on him again.

"Um, Jolie?" He winced at the hesitant sound of his voice. Especially when she pretended not to hear him.

A windblown strand of sun-kissed brown hair curved against her cheek. Dusty stopped himself from brushing it back around her ear or tucking it into the French braid neatly fastened at the back of her head.

"Spit it out, Dusty."

He blinked a couple of times, as if to verify that she'd actually spoken to him. She laid the knife on the counter, then wiped her hands on a towel. She turned cloudy blue eyes on him. "I've already accepted that I'm not going to like what you have to say, so just be out with it."

"Uh…" Grand sakes alive, he felt like a speechless teenager all over again. There was something about the thin black that encircled her irises. The direct way she looked at him and only him. The enticing way she discreetly caught the inner flesh of her bottom lip that shot his best intentions all to hell.

The widening of her pupils told him that the effect was fully mutual. All at once the stiffness around her jaw eased, and he was afraid she was a heartbeat away from bestowing on him one of those all-Jolie smiles that would undoubtedly knock him down for the count.

Before he could question the wisdom, he reached out and gently worked a single white chicken feather from her hair. Her intake of breath was so shallow he was certain he was the only one who heard it. He slowly pulled his hand back, displaying the feather. "Um, a little remnant from your run."

Her cheeks colored, then her gaze dropped suggestively to his mouth. She blinked. "You shaved off your mustache."

Dusty lifted a hand to his bare upper lip. "Yeah."

His own gaze lingered on her just-moistened lips. If she didn't stop looking at him like that, more would be sizzling than just the steaks.

With incredible self-restraint, Dusty hauled his gaze from Jolie's mouth. He switched off the burner under the nearly melted potatoes, wondering just how he went about switching off the flame in his gut.

Just be out with it, indeed.

"Jolie...I've come to pick up the divorce papers."

For the life of her, Jolie couldn't figure out why she felt as if she'd just lopped a finger off with the knife. In the time she'd avoided coming into the kitchen she'd pretty

much figured out that the reason Dusty had come back was
not a good one. She merely hadn't taken the assumption
to the next step and connected his presence with the
unsigned papers she'd stuck into a drawer at home the
instant she received them a couple of months back.

Which was stupid, really. And that only agitated her
further. She'd spent her life proving that she was the
exact opposite of stupid. Up to any task set in front of
her, she was. A regular anything-you-can-do-I-can-do-
just-as-well kind of girl, with her feet firmly steeped in
reality. She'd had to be for her own survival. It hadn't
been easy being raised by a paternal grandfather who
didn't have a clue on how to react to a six-year-old girl,
much less raise one. As he'd told her often enough, he'd
seen to raising his one son and that should be more than
any one man should have to endure. So Jolie had learned
at a young age how to not only look after herself, but after
him. Seemed she was always trying to keep placated the
well-meaning but nosy townsfolk who questioned the
old man's ability to look after her. For they were at the
ready to take her away from the only family she had left.

Of course, no one was happier than she was when the
time finally came for her to start making her own decisions. And nothing had intrigued her like the beast that
had stolen her parents from her: fire.

"Jolie?"

She blinked Dusty's handsome face back into focus,
noting the pity there. She hated that he felt sorry for her.
That hadn't always been the case. Of course, when you
were six years old and the older next-door neighbor
was paying you attention, you didn't recognize that

same attention as pity. You just took attention any way you could get it.

Now she knew better.

"They're…um, the papers are back at the house."

"I see."

She gathered the salad fixings into a bowl and tossed them. "You didn't think I kept them here in my locker, did you?"

His half grin made her remember that mischievous boy who used to include her in all the goings-on. "Let's put it this way—it wouldn't have surprised me."

She realized then that the room had gotten suspiciously quiet. She turned to find the poker game going on as if in slow motion. Her cheeks flamed. How much of her conversation with Dusty had they overheard? She hadn't told a soul that she'd heard from Dusty, much less received divorce papers from him. Heck of a way for them to find out.

Who was she kidding? She was probably the last person in town to figure out he wasn't coming back when he left.

She cleared her throat. "Okay, guys, wrap it up. Dinner's on."

A flurry of activity followed, though any attempt at conversation was awkward at best. She began to set the table alongside Martinez when Dusty grasped her wrist.

Her pulse gave a telltale leap and her throat went as dry as charred wood. Which was silly, really. His touch was meant as nothing more than a halting measure.

Yeah, tell that to her body.

"Jolie?"

She looked to where everyone was nearly settled

around the table. "Look, Dusty, can we talk about this later?"

The sound of the alarm sliced through the room, eliciting a series of groans and curses. Three bells. That meant they needed both engines, which would nearly empty out the firehouse.

"Figures," Gary groaned. "First decent meal we've had around here in six months and I can't even eat it."

He along with a couple of the other men stuffed what they could into their mouths and pockets, then rushed out of the room to grab their gear.

Jolie started after them, feeling almost relieved. Talk about being saved by the bell. Although she was certain that whoever had coined the phrase hadn't had quite this interruption in mind.

"Jolie," Dusty said again, more insistently.

She turned to face him, and nearly tripped over Spot for the second time that day. She looked down to make sure the cat was okay, wondering just what exactly was going on in her little feline brain. She received an irritated twitch of a black tail for her effort as the cat scampered off into the station.

Jolie flicked her gaze back to Dusty. His expectant expression tightened the vise around her heart. For a second she'd forgotten where they were, where she was, thinking he'd be on her heels, rushing for the nearest engine right along with her.

But he wasn't. And probably never would be again.

She dug her fingers into her front jeans pocket. "Here," she said, tossing him her house keys. "Stay at the house. I'll see you at eight tomorrow morning."

Chapter 2

Jolie gazed wistfully at the autumn sun hovering on the horizon. She wished the weak rays could chase away the cold that seemed to chill the marrow of her bones. It had been an especially grueling twenty-four-hour shift. Only she wasn't convinced her work schedule was the cause of her reluctance to walk the six blocks home. No, she knew it wasn't. The dragging of her feet had more to do with the man who was waiting at the end of her walk. Her husband. The man who had walked out on her and their marriage without a second glance. A man who had returned. For whatever reasons.

Jolie felt…well, strange, was the best way she could describe it. For so long now, she had grown accustomed to being on her own. Living a compartmentalized existence. At work she was still part of a team, a family, really, where there was little time to ponder her marriage, her life, and what, if anything, she could do to change either.

When she attended town events, or went shopping, she was the same person she'd always been. Or so she tried to convince everyone. And, just being around others made her feel that maybe in some ways she was.

It wasn't until she went home after her regular twenty-four-hour shift, then spent the next two days there waiting for her next shift, or returned from grocery shopping or lunch with her best friend and sister-in-law, Darby, that she became aware all over again of the void that was her life. A void that had gaped open the instant Dusty had told her he couldn't live with her anymore.

Petition for Divorce.

Shivering, Jolie worked her hand through a too-long denim coat sleeve, then tucked her hair behind her ear.

She didn't know what hurt her more. The fact that Dusty was seeking a divorce. Or that he had personally come back to compel her to agree to it.

The brisk morning air burned her eyes. At least that's what she told herself as she blinked back tears and picked up her pace. She decided that Dusty's seeking a divorce bothered her more than his being back, however temporarily. Their marriage, their life together, had been more real than anything to her. Being with him had filled her with a hope, a hunger for living, a sheer happiness that she couldn't remember feeling before. Not since her parents were ripped from her life when she was six. He'd made her feel loved. Needed. As if she belonged.

Which left her wondering what she was supposed to be feeling now.

Of course, she and Dusty had been unable to have children....

Jolie bit solidly on her bottom lip, emotionally incapable of probing that raw wound. Not on top of everything else swirling inside her right now.

The one person she had shared part of her ordeal with was Pastor Adams. He had asked if she'd like him to intervene on her behalf. Contact Dusty and try to talk things out with him. She'd not only declined his offer, she'd taken his suggestion as almost an insult. It was bad enough that she hadn't been woman enough to keep her man. Now she needed a clergyman to intercede on her behalf? Go after her missing husband and beg for him to come back? She let the pastor know in so many words that she'd rather eat a bucket full of earthworms first, a feeling that hadn't changed even after crying for two days straight after her conversation with him. And not even after his sermon on pride.

Pride. Now there was a word. What was a woman to do when it seemed that pride was all that made her get up in the morning? That saw her through living in a house still chock-full of her husband's presence? Injected the very fire she fought into her veins whenever she caught one of the townsfolk looking at her in that long, pitying way?

She rounded the corner and the small two-story renovated farmhouse came into view. In the driveway parked behind her Jeep was Dusty's pickup. Of course she'd known he'd be there. But actually seeing him there was another matter entirely.

Mrs. Noonan across the street opened her screen door with a telling squeak. Jolie fought the urge to roll her eyes. Awfully coincidental that the town's busiest busybody chose this moment to collect a morning paper delivered two hours ago.

"'Morning, Jolie!" she called out.

Jolie waved a hand and returned the greeting.

"I see you've sold the house."

Sold…the…house…

Jolie's gaze edged the neat front lawn, then traveled to where only a hole indicated that there was once a Realtor's sign posted. Her stomach tightened. Dusty must have taken it down when he'd come home last night.

Home. She'd have to stop referring to it as such. The house they'd spent five years in together was no longer home. Not to him. Not to her.

"I'm sure it's a mistake, Mrs. Noonan. The house hasn't been sold." *Yet.*

Collecting the morning paper, she instinctively reached for her keys, only then remembering that she'd given them to Dusty the night before. Resting her palm against the smooth wood door, she thought she'd rather break a window than have to knock to get into a place that had been hers alone for the past few months. She curved her fingers around the doorknob. It turned easily in her grasp. She gave a faint gasp of relief and pushed it inward.

As she closed the door behind her, she instantly became aware of the proof that someone other than herself was in the house. The aroma of coffee wafting from the kitchen. Hiking boots abandoned in the hall.

Papers strewn across the coffee table while the television mutely flickered the morning news.

Jolie caught herself tiptoeing and censured herself. What was she afraid of?

"Dusty?" she called out, dropping the paper and her purse on the hall table and craning her neck to peek through the kitchen doorway. He didn't answer. She forced herself to walk into the room, feeling as if something were different. The yellow walls seemed... brighter, somehow. Refusing to explore the reasons for that, and especially not daring to think Dusty's presence the cause, she took a mug from the cupboard and poured herself a cup of coffee from the half-full carafe. She eyed the dark sludge. Not exactly fresh. Shrugging out of the coat she had on, she draped it on the back of a slatted wood chair, then lingered over it, running her fingers down the well-worn denim. She absently plucked a couple of Spot's white hairs from the material. Since the mornings had turned brisk a couple of weeks ago, she'd taken to wearing the wool-lined jacket Dusty had left behind. She supposed he'd be taking it along with the divorce papers and the rest of his stuff when he left again.

Thrusting the thought from her mind, she turned toward the counter and set about making a fresh pot of coffee. She filled the water reservoir then scooped in the grounds. A loud banging noise from upstairs startled her. She crossed her arms over her chest and stared warily at the ceiling. What was he doing?

The coffee couldn't brew fast enough for her. Halfway through the cycle, she quickly poured two cups, then headed for the stairs. A splash of white on the gleaming oak kitchen table slowed her steps, then drew her to a stop. Dusty had laid out their divorce papers.

She didn't have to ask how he'd found them. She had a habit of shoving everything into a desk drawer as she received the items, planning to get to them later. Only in this case "later" hadn't come soon enough for him.

The banging upstairs started up again. Her heart beating an uneven rhythm in her chest, she climbed the stairs and followed the sounds through the second-floor hall. Her palms grew instantly damp as she realized he was working on the master bath. Correction, the half of a master bath. Dusty had begun the addition about a year ago and had left it unfinished, much as he'd left their relationship unfinished.

Her knees as firm as an empty fire hose, she stepped into the bedroom, *her* bedroom, and stood frozen before the rumpled four-poster bed. A bed she had slept in alone for the past six months. A bed Dusty had obviously slept in last night.

She tightened her fingers on the coffee mugs, afraid she might drop them. There were at least two other places he could have chosen to sleep. One a comfortable guest bedroom, two, the oversize couch downstairs. Why had he chosen her bed?

The sound of hammering resumed and she forced herself to the half-open door that led off to the left. From a discarded leather tool belt, to a greasy rag, then a piece of floor molding, her gaze wandered until it settled on the back of Dusty's jeans. The faded material hugged his athletic thighs and legs to perfection.

Despite everything, Jolie found herself awkwardly attracted to her husband.

"You read my mind."

Her gaze flickered to Dusty's wryly smiling face, then to the tipping cups she still held. She quickly righted them, nearly causing the liquid to spill out the other way.

She shakily handed him his cup.

He took a hefty sip. "Just as I like it. Heavy on the coffee."

Grasping her own cup in both hands, she looked at him. Really looked at him for the first time since she'd spotted him at the firehouse yesterday. God, but he looked better than any one man had the right to. His light brown hair was as closely cropped as ever, making her palms itch with the need to run them slowly over the spiky strands. His rich Irish-cream brown eyes were just as watchful, making her feel as though he looked straight through the wall of her chest and into her heart. His body was just as defined, the six-pack ripple of his stomach muscles clearly visible under his chest-hugging white T-shirt, his hips just as trim beneath his close-fitting jeans.

"What…what are you doing?" she asked, surprised by the gravelly sound of her voice.

He put his cup aside, then wiped his mouth with a slow, long sweep of his wrist. He gestured toward the Jacuzzi. "I, um, woke up early and thought I'd have a go at finishing this."

Jolie swallowed hard. This was all too comfort-able…too normal, when everything between them was everything but. "You don't have to do that."

"I know."

Before she could stop herself, she asked the question that had been burning on her tongue ever since he'd voluntarily placed himself within shouting distance. Drawing a shaky breath, she asked, "Dusty, where have you been?"

Dusty sat back on his heels as though pushed back. The inside of his eyelids felt peppered with sand, reminding him how very little he'd slept last night. Looking at the smudges under Jolie's eyes, he guessed she hadn't fared any better. But while she'd had the firehouse to keep her busy, he'd been stuck at the house with little more to do than think about everything that had come before. Everything that would come after.

He glanced around the half-finished room, the only place in the entire house that hadn't been there since the beginning of time. He knew every inch of this place. Just which floorboards would creak when you stepped on them. Which windows you could jimmy open with a couple of jostled tries even when locked. The slight incline of the kitchen floor from where the house had settled. Not perceptible to the human eye, but obvious when you spilled something and the liquid pooled near the back door as if seeking a way out.

Somewhere around 4:00 a.m., after he'd found the divorce papers crammed at the very bottom of the desk drawer, then watched TV until he'd overdosed on infomercials, he'd drifted off to sleep on the couch only to awaken with a start a little while later. Without thinking, he'd dragged himself upstairs and dropped into the bed they had once shared. It wasn't until after he was surrounded by Jolie's sweet lemony scent, and after he'd had an especially steamy dream that left him drenched in sweat, that he'd given up on catching any quality shut-eye, fixed himself some coffee, then headed back upstairs to check out what she had done with the master bath. It didn't take long to figure out that she'd done nothing. The door had been tightly closed, his tools were still out exactly where he'd left them. It was almost as if he'd stopped working a day or two ago and had returned to finish the job. Never left.

But he had left. And though some things hadn't changed, many other things had.

Deciding to avoid her question, he asked one of his own. "When did you put the house up for sale?"

Her gaze flitted away from his to settle on the cup she held. She gave a casual shrug of her shoulders, but the straight way she held herself told him she felt anything but casual. "Last month."

He cocked a brow. "Don't you think it would have been a good idea to ask me first?"

"I did ask you. When your attorney called a couple months back I asked him what you wanted me to do with the house. He told me that you wanted me to have it."

"I meant that you should stay here."

She gazed at him for a long moment before answering. "Why?" she asked quietly. "This is your family's house, not mine. I wasn't raised here, Dusty. If you didn't care about…what happens with it, why should I?" She leaned against the jamb. "Where'd you put the sign?"

He hooked a thumb toward the window. "Out back. I chopped it for kindling."

Her eyes widened. "You didn't."

"I most certainly did. Though I doubt the Realtor will be very happy with my actions, it sure as hell made me feel a lot better about the whole thing."

The sound of strangled laughter surprised him. And inspired a grin of his own. He'd thought she'd be upset. Although judging by her own expression, she was just as shocked as he was by her reaction.

"You know, I really shouldn't be amused by this," she said. "I should be absolutely livid that you've come back and taken over just like you'd never…"

He scanned her features, noticing the way her lips were slightly parted, as if she were ready to breathe the last word but didn't dare. "Like I never left?"

Jolie stood completely silent for a couple of heart-beats, the amusement shifting from her face. She abruptly turned, pretending to take a sip of her coffee, though he suspected her throat was as open to liquids as his was, and that was not at all.

"You didn't have to come back for the papers, you know," she finally said, placing her mug on the unfinished sink and turning to face him. "You could have just had your attorney call my attorney and remind him." She hugged herself, the unconscious action making his own arms ache to hold her. "Remind me."

As Dusty watched her shut herself off from him, he reminded himself that her emotional distance wasn't a result of his leaving. It was one of the things that had propelled him to leave.

He mindlessly gathered his tools together and pushed to his feet. "I suppose I could have done that." He faced her. "If I thought calling would have had a chance in hell of working, I would have." He stepped closer to her. "Admit it, Jolie. When you stuck those papers into the drawer, you did so with no intention of signing them."

The way she blinked told him he was right. Jolie had never been very good at bluffing. Once upon a time, everything she felt, everything she thought, had been all right there on her lovely face for all to see. And right now he saw a woman bursting with a pain felt so deeply it reached out and enveloped him in its dark fingers. The emotion was the first honest one he'd seen from her in so long that it nearly knocked his knees out from under him.

"Oh, Jolie, the last thing I ever wanted to do was hurt you."

Her brows drew together and her voice was low when she spoke. "How did you think I would feel when you left, Dusty? Filed for a…divorce? Did you think I'd be happy?"

He grimaced. She'd likely felt the same way he had after he'd lost his brother, Erick, six months ago to the same kind of fire she fought nearly every day. A loss that had changed his life. Made him realize the importance of life period. "Of course I didn't—"

"Please explain it to me, because right now I'm not understanding a whole lot. If you didn't want to hurt me, then why did you leave? If you didn't want to hurt me, then why did you send me divorce papers? If you didn't want to hurt me, then why—" her voice caught "—why did you come back?"

"Aw, Jolie…"

Dusty wasn't sure of the logistics, but suddenly his arms were full of Jolie. Sweet, soft, wonderful Jolie. Her fresh-smelling hair tickled his nose. Her breasts pressed against his chest. Her back was as rigid as all get out, and he was the only one doing all the holding, but right that minute it didn't matter.

Given the way things had been between them in the end, he'd had no idea his leaving had hurt Jolie so deeply. So irreparably. She had always been so strong. Taken everything in stride. He'd thought she'd be relieved when he left. For the first time in five years of marriage she could lead her life the way she wanted without someone questioning what she was doing. All she was putting at risk every time she walked out that door and went to the fire station.

Hadn't she grown tired of their arguments? Hadn't she had enough of their going nose-to-nose at the dinner table until every last bit of their appetites left them?

"Aw, hell, Jolie," he said, burrowing his nose into her hair and whispering into her ear. "I've never stopped wanting you."

She drew back, her blue, blue eyes nearly swallowed by tears. It was all he could do not to kiss her then. To claim her trembling lips with his. To mold her compact little body to his. To show her with actions how very much he wanted her even now.

Her gaze dropped to his mouth and he nearly groaned, immediately pegging the gesture for what it was. She wanted to be kissed as much as he wanted to kiss her. And he knew in that instant that he was going to do it, consequences be damned.

A brief touch. That's all. He'd brush his mouth against hers, then pull away.

The instant his lips made contact with hers, her tear-damp ones softened under his. Dusty groaned. Okay, maybe he should broaden the kiss parameters a tad. Say full contact for no more than ten seconds. As if on its own hungry accord, his tongue dipped out and gently lapped her salty tears. Whoa, that wasn't supposed to happen. But, oh, she tasted so good. Jolie swayed against him, her arms curving around his waist, her fingers digging into the small of his back near his spine. In that one lucid moment, he knew he was a goner.

A brief touch melted into a needful seeking as he slid his tongue into the hot, honeyed depths of her mouth. Everything might have been all right if she hadn't re-sponded. But she had—in a breathless, thirsty way that sent his blood surging hotly through his veins like the fires they'd spent so much of their lives fighting. It was all Dusty could do not to back her against the edge of the unfinished Jacuzzi, push her sweater up over her ribs and pop open the button to her snug jeans….

Just like old times.

The thought caught and held. Just like old times. Only it wasn't old times, was it? No matter how right she felt in his arms right now, the emotions she had mo-mentarily bared to him, how much he wanted to take their kiss to the next level, nothing was the same.

He purposefully set her away from him, his hands a little rough on her arms. "Jolie, this…isn't a good idea."

She drew a shaky hand across her parted, well-kissed lips, looking as shocked as he felt. "No. No, it isn't." She stepped a little farther back away from him. "I'm sorry…I don't know what came over me. I guess I'm tired. And—"

"Don't blame yourself, Jolie. If anyone's to blame, it's me." He gave her a halfhearted smile. "Though your cooperation didn't help matters much."

She dropped her hand to her side and returned his smile. "Good thing one of us is thinking clearly, huh?"

He looked away. He may have stopped himself before things spiraled out of control, but Dusty was far from describing his thoughts as clear. If he didn't get out of this room, put some major distance between himself and Jolie *now,* it wouldn't take a whole lot for him to sweep her up into his arms and carry her to the bed in the other room.

Jolie picked up her coffee cup. "I'd better go get some sleep. Maybe after…" Her gaze locked onto his. "Will you be around for a couple more hours?"

He wanted to tell her no, he needed to leave now. But his simple mission had swelled into a complicated one. He needed to stay and work those complications out. As much for Jolie's sake as for his own.

He finally nodded. "Yeah. I will." He reached out and tucked a stray strand of her hair behind a tiny ear. "You go on. I'll be here."

For now.

The words couldn't have been louder if he had shouted them, though he was pretty sure he hadn't even said them aloud.

Chapter 3

*D*umb, *dumb, dumb, dumb.* Dusty paced restlessly across the length of the living room, then back again, his every instinct wanting to lead him to the stairs and up to where Jolie lay in the bed they had once shared together.

Knowing he'd either end up in that bed with her—if she'd have him—or go crazy keeping himself away from her, he snatched up his jacket and headed for the front door. It was only when his booted feet pounded against the pavement, the crisp autumn air whisking by his ears, that his thoughts were no longer dictated by the longings of his body.

What had he done, kissing her like that? He had no right to touch her, much less take liberties with her mouth, no matter how tempted he'd been. He'd given up that right months ago.

So why was it he wanted for all the world to reclaim that right?

None of this made sense. The instant he rolled back into town, he'd felt as if he'd been gone five minutes. His old friends warmly welcomed him back, no questions asked. Every memory he'd ever formed in the small, quirky town had come flooding back. And his feelings for Jolie seemed to have grown more acute rather than diminishing, as he would have guessed.

He reminded himself that his reasons for leaving Jolie had nothing to do with not loving her anymore. Rather, they had more to do with her loving something more than him that he could no longer compete with.

He groaned, still practically able to taste Jolie on his tongue. Aching with need for her.

Hormones run amok, he told himself. It was as simple as that.

Simple. There was that damn word again. *Simple* didn't come near describing a single event of this trip. He'd expected to waltz into town, get the divorce papers signed, then waltz right back out again, ready to restart his life from scratch. Allow Jolie to do the same.

Instead he'd hung out at the fire station, stayed the night in Jolie's sweet-smelling bed, resumed work on the master bath, and nearly molested her the first time they were left alone.

Smooth move, Conrad.

There was nothing like further confusing the issue than…further confusing the issue.

And if he'd really only planned to stay a couple hours, why had he taken a week off work?

He was so occupied by his thoughts he had no idea where he was heading. Until his feet stopped and he found himself staring at the ironwork archway leading into the town's only cemetery.

He grimaced and rubbed the back of his neck. It was as though his subconscious had sensed his need for reinforcement, and the death of his brother was definitely that.

Dusty stood there for long moments, absently watching colorful leaves flutter from the tall oaks flanking the gate, then swirl lazily along the path. To say that losing Erick had been the beginning of the end of his marriage might be overstating things, but his brother's death was the one event that had set everything that came after into motion.

With slow, measured steps, he walked into the plainly laid-out cemetery, sticking to the cobblestone pathway barely wide enough to hold a car. For two hundred years this is where the townsfolk were laid to rest. It had only seemed natural that Erick should be buried here, as well.

The quiet hum of an engine sounded behind him, forcing him up onto the grass as a funeral procession drove slowly by. He watched the flagged cars, clearly remembering the cool spring day he'd buried Erick. Twenty-eight years old. Far too young for a life to be snuffed out.

Finally, he stood before the chest-high marble stone that reflected his brother's name. It was difficult to reconcile the cold etching with the zealous man Erick had been. Beloved Husband, Father, Son and Brother, it read.

His gaze caught on something at the base. He leaned over and picked up a shiny red toy fire truck.

His fingers tightened around the tiny metal frame. He'd been in phone contact with his brother's widow about once a month since he'd left. When he'd decided to come back, an important item on his agenda was to stop by to see Darby at her sprawling ranch on the outskirts of town. See how she was truly doing with his own two eyes and if she really didn't need the help he tried to extend to her. To say hi and breathe in the little-girl smell of his twin six-year-old nieces who resembled Erick so much it hurt just looking at them.

He was sure that one of the girls, or maybe even Darby herself, had left the toy fire engine. He rubbed his thumb along the painted side, the toy reminding him of one he and Erick used to fight over when they were younger. When their father headed off for one of his twenty-four-hour shifts and he and his brother would sit on the front step watching him go, rooster-proud that their father was a firefighter. Wanting nothing more than to grow up so they could become firefighters themselves.

Firefighting was a Conrad tradition. Their father, his father before him, and his grandfather before then, the tradition reached back to the time the town was settled. It was only natural that Dusty, himself, would apply at the firehouse the instant he graduated community college and was old enough to enroll. Dusty smiled grimly, remembering how soundly jealous Erick had been that he'd gotten to go first. Erick had probably hated their age difference in that one moment more than he had at any other time in their lives.

Not that Erick's age had kept him away from the station. Or even from following the truck out on runs.

Scott Wahl's face flashed in Dusty's mind and he shook his head, wondering if firefighting was some sort of disease. And if it was, if there was a foolproof cure.

A hundred feet away, the funeral attendants were getting out of their cars. The sun glinted off the maple coffin where six pallbearers lifted it from the back of the hearse. He instantly recognized John Sparks as one of those men, though he was wearing civilian clothes rather than his sheriff's uniform. He squinted at the others gathered, recognizing most of them, although the pastor was unfamiliar. Definitely not Pastor Adams. He wondered who had passed away. Then he remembered John saying something about Violet Jenkins being found elbow deep in dirt, planting tulip bulbs in her garden a couple of days ago. He rubbed his closed eyelids. God, Mrs. Jenkins had seemed ancient when he was a kid. He wondered how old she'd ended up living to.

The thought immediately led to the young age of Erick when Dusty had lost the battle with the fire that took his brother's life.

He stood numbly, staring at the headstone.

"Dusty."

He looked up to find John Sparks standing a few feet away, his suit jacket swung over his shoulder, his other hand in his pants pocket. He couldn't be sure how long he'd stood there, but a glance around told him it must have been a while, for the place was nearly deserted.

"Sparky."

John took that as an okay to come closer. He stepped up next to Dusty and both of them stood looking at Erick's grave.

"You know, he's probably up there now getting a big kick out of us both standing together like this mourning over him."

Dusty shifted a glance toward the too bright autumn sky. He grinned. "Yeah, he probably is."

John folded his jacket over his forearm. "So what brings you here?"

Dusty looked at him. "What do you mean?"

The younger man shrugged. "Well, rumor has it you stayed at Jolie's...er, your old place last night." His grin was decidedly suggestive. "I would have thought you and she would, um, be catching up on old times."

Dust bent down and put the toy fire truck back where he'd found it. If only Sparks knew how close to the truth that statement came to describing what had happened between him and Jolie this morning.

John held up his hands. "Trust me, I'm not looking for details. It's hard enough being a single guy and working with a woman who looks like Jolie *without* knowing the details." His chuckle was light.

Dusty straightened. "Who's the new pastor?"

John stared at him, probably recognizing the change in subject for what it was. Dusty didn't know what Jolie had told everyone, but he was guessing it wasn't much given their co-workers' response to his being back. For whatever reason, she hadn't shared the truth with any of them. And it wasn't up to him to tell them. Long after he had gone, Jolie would have to live here. Better she should handle things the way she saw fit.

"He's not new, really. Just temporary. You know, while Pastor Adams is on a pilgrimage to Lourdes. He said it was the first time the collections were enough for him to make the trip and he was damn well going to use every cent of it."

Dusty grinned. "Sounds like Adams."

"Jonas is the name of the fill-in. Jonas Noble. They say he's from Montana, but nobody knows for sure. He doesn't much like to talk about himself."

"Ah, he's got the gossips' tongues to wagging, has he?" Good. That left them with less time to try to pick apart his and Jolie's crumbling marriage.

"Wagging? If you could channel the energy the towns-folk generate, we'd never pay for another electric bill."

The two of them chuckled. Then they both fell silent and turned their attention back to the headstone.

"I miss him, you know?" Sparks said quietly.

Dusty nodded. He missed his brother, too. More than he could say.

John cleared his throat. "I've, um, been out to Darby's a couple times. You know, to see if she needs any work done around the house and stuff. Figured Erick would have wanted me to keep an eye out for her and all."

Dusty nodded. "How's she's doing?"

"As well as can be expected, I guess. As independent as all get out. Wouldn't even let me take out the garbage. And trust me, with all those damn animals she's got out there, there's a lot of it." He frowned, then looked off into the distance. "I get the impression she blames Erick for what happened."

Dusty digested the information. What would Darby do if she knew the blame rested solely on him? "I think that's only natural. She never much liked Erick's passion for his job." *Just like he could no longer stomach Jolie's obsession with hers.*

"What about the girls?" he asked.

"Couldn't tell you anything there. They don't seem to like me much." It slightly startled Dusty when John dropped an arm over his shoulders. "Everyone should be gathering at Eddie's for a drink about now. What do you say we head over and tie one on? You know, for old times' sake."

Dusty thought of Jolie back at the house, lying in the middle of that old bed. Visualized the tangle of her rich brown hair spilled across the pillow. Imagined her sleep-warm skin....

He cleared his throat. "Yeah. Um, lead on."

It was only twelve o'clock, but he was willing to do something, anything, to keep from going back to the house, climbing those stairs and slipping into bed with Jolie.

Chapter 4

Jolie fingered through the fresh greens in the produce corner of Old Jake's General Store, passing her own favorite of collard and going for the dandelion that Dusty always liked so much. Curling her fingers into her palm, she pulled back her hand altogether, then pushed the cart toward the tomatoes.

The past half hour had been spent doing exactly the same thing. She'd reach for an item, then something would catch her eye and she'd automatically reroute to finger a choice Dusty would favor. The items in her cart totaled four. Laundry detergent, flour, sugar and milk. Generic items that didn't have any connection to Dusty.

Well, okay, maybe she preferred that specific brand of detergent because she loved the way it smelled on

Dusty's clothes where they rested against his skin. But no one but her need know that.

In the three hours since Dusty had left the house after kissing her, she'd tried to sleep, but failed. Scrubbed the kitchen floor to exhaust herself, and still was wide awake. Then she resigned herself to the fact that she wasn't going to get the rest she needed after twenty-four hours at the firehouse. It was a good thing she'd stolen a couple of hours' rest between calls late last night or else she'd be dead on her feet right about now.

Not that her current emotional state was any improvement. She picked through the tomatoes, then chose a bunch of green lettuce. Even now her nerve endings seemed to tingle, jolted awake by Dusty's skillful kiss and refusing to lie still. Her muscles were tense, her lips still felt swollen...and her body cried out for more than the brief, fevered contact. Not even running errands had been successful in banishing the unwanted feelings. But it had added a decidedly sharper edge to them and her reaction.

When she'd set off in her Jeep, she'd conveniently forgotten the smallness of the town and the open curiosity of the townsfolk. No matter how well-meaning they were, they were downright nosy now that word of Dusty's return had gotten around. She'd kept busy enough at the station that she hadn't heard much from her fellow firefighters. But Madge at the post office had been another matter. Then there'd been Gene at the combination dry cleaners-launderette. On top of that, Roger at the gas station had rested a hand against the rooftop of her Jeep and grinned down at her while the pump automatically filled the tank and asked why she didn't look more cheerful, what with Dusty being back and all.

"Jolie? Jolie Calbert Conrad, is that you?"

Jolie tightened her hands on the cart handle, filled with the incredible urge to run. She wouldn't have stopped at the general store at all except that she was out of the essentials and had to. She'd known before going in that the central town gossiping center, second only to Eddie's pub, was a minefield of astronomic proportions. In fact, she was surprised she'd gotten through a half hour of shopping without someone approaching her.

Carefully fastening a smile onto her tired features, she turned toward Elva Mollenkopf. "Hi, Elva. Doing some shopping?"

Yes, the question was mundane, but sometimes when you stated the obvious, the other person dove into a monologue on what they were buying and why.

Not Elva. Her almost predatory smile made Jolie want to set the cart wheels spinning, then jump on the foot rest and let it carry her away.

"Is it true?" Elva asked.

Jolie blinked. "Is what true?"

"Is Dusty really back…and staying at the house?"

Jolie swallowed hard against the cotton batting in her throat. She debated saying something along the lines of "It's not what you think," or even toyed with the idea of saying "It's none of your business," but she gauged that neither would go over real well with the woman who was twenty years her senior.

"It's true," someone said, but Jolie was pretty sure it wasn't her. She turned her head to see Angela Johansen approaching from behind. Of course, her last name had once been Paglio, back in grade and high school when Jolie had shared more than a few classes with her. They'd always been friends, though not the type of call-every-day, tell-all-your-secrets-to kind of friends.

They had, however, always been there to back each other up.

"Hi, Jolie," Angie said with a warm, knowing smile. "How are you, Elva?" she said a little coolly. "It's good to see you again. I don't think our paths have crossed since…well, God, since the Fourth of July celebration when you had that mishap with Joe Johnson's dogs. How is your leg, anyway?"

Jolie's gaze settled on the little blond-haired girl in the seat of Angela's cart. Angela's daughter with her husband Jeff should be all of five about now. Eleanor's chubby fingers were working to free a hard candy from its wrapper, her face contorted in concentration. Jolie's heart automatically contracted, the way it did whenever she came across a child of the age hers might have been. Had she and Dusty had kids.

Saying something to Elva that Jolie didn't quite catch, Angela linked her arm with Jolie's and determinedly turned her, leading her and her cart away from Elva.

Angela leaned closed to her. "I still think she's a vampire," she whispered.

Jolie laughed quietly, sneaking a glance over her shoulder to find Elva staring after them in dumbfounded silence. "God, I forgot about that. How old were we when that rumor circulated through school?"

"Eight, maybe? But that doesn't matter. While I no

longer think Elva goes around sucking people's blood, I do think she feeds on others' hardships." She grimaced. "Always at the ready to sink her teeth into any festering wounds."

Jolie smiled at little Eleanor, her words aimed for Angela. "Maybe it's the only way she can make it through the day. You know, compare her life to others' and be glad that she doesn't have the problems that we do."

Ellie's wide blue eyes were firmly on her mother. "Mommy, what's a vampire?"

Angela laughed and chucked the little girl under her dimpled chin. "Never you mind, sweet pea. Do you want some Cocoa Puffs?"

Jolie appreciated Angela's deft handling of the awkward question, wondering if she could have handled a similar situation so well with her own kids. If she had kids.

Angela stopped her cart and placed a box of the sugary cereal into her full cart much to Ellie's delight. She searched the area around them. "I think the coast is clear."

Jolie smiled her thanks at her friend. Not just for saving her from a humiliating incident with Elva…but for not asking about Dusty herself. As Angela walked away, she reminded herself to call her later in the week so they could have some coffee together or something. It had been some time since they'd played catch-up.

Of course, Angela was nowhere to be found when Kathy, the cashier, Justin, the manager, then Ruth, whose chickens she had rescued yesterday, all assailed her with questions. Kathy was well-meaning, Justin was looking for tawdry details; while Ruth offered up some advice on how to guarantee Dusty wouldn't leave again. Advice involving chicken fat and feathers that made Jolie shudder.

Finally, she sat behind the wheel of her Jeep, the door tightly closed and locked, her breathing sounding much too ragged in the empty SUV.

It wasn't that the questions got to her. It was more that they were far too similar to the questions swirling in her own mind. Clamoring for answers that only one person could give her. Answers she was beginning to fear she'd never get.

She switched on the ignition and waited for the heater to warm the interior of the SUV.

Where her nerves had been a mess after Dusty had kissed her mere hours before, now they visually shook with the tension further created by her outing. When he'd left, the world as she knew it had ended. It had taken her a long time just to be able to get up in the morning, face her friends and co-workers, function like more than a robot, her heart bearing scars she didn't dare show anyone.

Then just like that Dusty was back and those wounds had been opened up afresh…and the townsfolk had more questions now than they had before.

Sometimes it seemed that all her life she'd been the oddity. The little girl whose parents had died in a fire and whose grandfather wasn't fit to raise her. She'd promised herself when she'd come of age that she'd never do anything again to garner such open attention.

And in all honesty, she hadn't this time, either. Dusty had.

She pushed her hair back from her face with shaking hands. Movement from the corner of her eyes vied for her attention and she glanced up from the dash to find Elva bearing down on her full speed, the wheels of her shopping cart wobbling ominously. Throwing the Jeep into reverse, Jolie squealed from the general store parking lot, nearly taking Elva's cart out in the process.

She honestly didn't know what more she could do, merely knew the desire to do something. Even though she'd tried to confront Dusty this morning. Asked him why he'd left. But he had skillfully avoided answering her.

What was there left to do?

"You can give him what he wants," she whispered.

The words seemed to echo in her ears. Her chest tightened to the point of pain.

What Dusty wanted was for her to sign the divorce papers.

She bit down so hard on her bottom lip she feared she'd drawn blood. In front of her, a low-slung sedan was going no more than ten miles an hour, the plates from a neighboring county. She forced herself to let up on the gas and follow at a safe distance, though the temptation to gun the engine and pass the out-of-towner was strong.

The downtown shops were all so very familiar. But rather than finding comfort in seeing Mrs. O'Malley tending to her autumn garden outside her bed-and-breakfast, and Penelope Moon hanging a sign advertising clearance prices on Halloween goodies, she saw threats looming everywhere. Mrs. O'Malley would tell her she'd been a fool. Penelope would probably say something along the lines of destiny had its own way of working things out and that she should just go with the flow, and would she like some aromatherapy candles to help see her through?

Jolie rubbed her throbbing temple as the car in front of her pulled to a stop. She halted as well, scanning the brick front of Eddie's pub. The day was warm enough that Eddie had the front door open, letting the early afternoon sun slant in and illuminate the first few stools. Her stomach dropped to the floorboard as she spotted Dusty sitting next to John Sparks and a couple of guys from the station.

The car in front of her finally moved, but she stayed completely still.

Almost as if sensing her presence, Dusty glanced up and through the door, his grin still firmly in place as his gaze collided with hers. His smile froze, then disappeared.

Give him what he wants, an inner voice taunted.

All she had to do was go back to the house. Sign the papers still lying on the kitchen table. Then hand them to him when he came back to the house.

Then again, she could just bring them down here and hand them to him along with his things. Or pin them to the front door and leave his stuff on the front porch.

John Sparks was questioning Dusty and he looked away, freeing her from his gaze.

Jolie's heart felt as if it might race right out of her chest as she carefully placed her foot on the gas. She knew in that instant that she had to do it. She had to give Dusty what he wanted. And she had to give it to him now.

* * *

Long strides took Dusty down the sidewalk of Main Street, his thoughts on everything but his surroundings. Until he turned the corner and the old house he'd grown up in loomed a block away. His heartbeat accelerated. His step slowed. His chest grew so tight it was difficult to breathe.

This was the only place he'd ever known as home. Every time he blinked, a different memory flashed through his mind, projections of images marked indelibly on his soul. The sprawling front lawn brought to mind Erick. How they would argue over whose turn it was to get the old mower out of the garage. Tussle in leaves that even now covered the lush green expanse. Toss a baseball back and forth, each lob growing a little harder, going a little farther, until his younger brother would purposely try to hit him with the ball.

But at the end of the day, just after dinner, before either of them were off to do whatever they had to do that night, he and Erick never failed to call a truce and meet as if by silent agreement on the front porch steps. They'd talk about everything. Or nothing at all. He'd always sat with his fingers clasped between his knees. Erick leaning back on his hands, staring off into some unforeseen future path that was mapped out for him in the sky.

Back then it seemed as if the day might never end. As if they'd had all the time in the world to tease each other about girlfriends. Debate which sports team was the better, the Detroit Tigers or the Cleveland Indians. Or just sit in quiet companionship while their mother

did the dinner dishes and their father either read the
paper at the kitchen table or was off at the firehouse.

Dusty reached those same steps and slowly sat down,
considering the view he'd seen a thousand times. Majestic oaks were at the height of color, setting the street
on fire with their oranges and yellows, their crisp smell
drifting on the air, prompting him to take a deep breath.
There didn't seem to be anything particularly unique
about the view itself. No. He presumed that he and his
brother had chosen this spot as their own because it was
neutral territory. Not his room. Not Erick's room. Not
their parents' room.

Of course eventually the entire house ended up his.
Yet sometimes it seemed as though this spot alone was
truly his. His and Erick's.

He looked down to find his hands clasped between
his knees. If only he'd been able to save Erick, this spot
would still be theirs.

"Are you going to marry her?" Erick's voice seemed
to drift to him on the cool autumn air, from some long-
ago, forgotten time.

Up until that point, the "m" word hadn't even entered
Dusty's mind. He and Erick had both been working at the
station by that point. And with their staggered shifts, it was
rare that they were both off at the same time. But they had
been that day. Before their parents sold him the house and
moved off to Arizona. Dusty had been dating Jolie for
barely a year by then. Erick had been dating Darby. And
his brother's question had nearly knocked him over.

Dusty snapped upright, much as he had that day.

"No," he'd said then, the idea so outrageous he

couldn't even imagine seriously considering it. Marriage was something people his parents' age did, not him. He was a fireman. Still lived at home.

"I don't know," he'd said moments later, the concept beginning to take root as he thought about the girl next door with the brown curly hair and big blue eyes who had transformed into all woman seemingly overnight. He couldn't even remember now why he hadn't asked her out before he had. But he suspected his motivations hadn't come totally from out of left field, and that Jolie had had a bit of a hand in his asking.

"Yes…I think I will." His slow answer had come after Erick hadn't responded, and then the concept had not only grown roots, the rightness had struck him, flowing through his veins as thickly as his own blood. Just as it had that day he'd met Jolie, when he'd picked her mail up from where she'd dropped it, her heather-blue eyes soft and sexy and all too inviting.

Dusty swallowed hard. He wondered what his brother would think of what was happening between him and Jolie now. He glanced toward that spot in the sky that Erick had always stared at, that unseen road that he wondered if he'd ever be able to view himself. A path Erick might be on even now.

Silently, he asked, "Erick, where are you? If ever I could have used your advice, it's now."

He sat for long moments, as if waiting for his brother to stroll from around the corner. Or for some bit of advice from the past to emerge in his mind that he could apply to the here and now. But nothing came. Only the dull, pulsating ache he always felt when he thought of

Erick. And how he had died six months ago because Dusty had been unable to save him.

He pushed off the steps and brushed his hands on the seat of his jeans. Almost as if in slow motion, he turned toward the door, for the first time in his life hesitating before opening it. He had to remember that this wasn't his home anymore. That the minute he'd left it six months ago, he'd given up all rights to coming and going without announcing himself, despite the weight of the key in his pocket.

But he and Jolie weren't divorced yet. And as long as he had a say in the matter, he wouldn't allow her to sell the place. He'd buy out her half if he had to and let it stand unoccupied before he let that happen.

With that thought in mind he moved his hand from where he'd been about to rap on the screen door and instead opened it and the inner door, entering the house as he had nearly every day of his life.

Instantly all that was familiar enveloped him. It was more than the scent of cinnamon that wafted to his nose from a bowl filled with some sort of flower mixture on the hall table; was something other than the collection of family photos that lined the walls, pictures his mother had left behind and that he and Jolie had had reframed and put back right where they were. It was everything combined that made him feel as if he was home.

Quietly closing the door against the autumn chill, he paused, then moved down the hall toward the back of the house. He knew where Jolie would be if she was home. She would be in the kitchen.

He rubbed the back of his neck. Funny, he hadn't

realized that he and Jolie had adopted his parents' behavior. That's exactly where he and Erick had gone after school, as much to see their mother, where she would be putting supper together, as to get a snack.

And that's where he found Jolie now, head bent over the table as she read something, the setting sun beaming through the window behind her and casting her silhouette in a warm yellow glow.

It wasn't all that long ago that his favorite pastime had been watching her when she didn't know he was there. It was confusing to know that that hadn't changed. That his longing to touch her soft hair was just as strong, maybe even stronger, than it had been before. That her curvy figure tempted his gaze just as it always had, from her small, high breasts and slender waist to the womanly flare of her hips. Even in a purple sweater and blue jeans and tennis shoes, she couldn't have been more beautiful had she been wearing that slinky black number she'd worn two Christmases ago. No, no, it had been New Year's Eve. And he'd been so hot for her he remembered slipping his hand up her toned thigh through the decadent slit up the side of the dress and stroking her to orgasm right there in the cab of his truck before going to the party the chief had held at the fire station.

He swallowed past the sudden tightness in his throat and fastened his gaze on her oval face. Her brows were pulled together in that way that told him she was doing something she didn't particularly like. Such as balancing the checkbook. Or paying the electric bill.

But he realized she wasn't doing either of those things. Rather, she was reading their divorce papers.

"I always hated when you watched me like that."

Her quietly said words wound around him, making him smile, if only slightly. "I know. Somehow I don't think that watching you would be half as fun if you did like it."

She looked up at him then, snaring him with her blue eyes, their shadowy depths as haunted as ever. And as irresistible.

She slowly turned the papers facedown on the table as if hiding what she'd been doing.

He didn't advance. He didn't retreat. He merely stood there looking at her, unsure as to what his next move should be. Or if he should make a move at all. Thinking perhaps he should wait for her to say something. To indicate what she'd been doing.

To ask him *why.*

Instead, she slowly got up from the table, slicing the sunlight as she moved toward the island on the other side of the kitchen and filled the coffeemaker with water and fresh grounds. He watched her, with every passing moment the silence growing thicker, his heartbeat growing louder.

"Dusty, is there…another woman?"

Her words were said so softly they were nearly drowned out by the catlike spitting and hissing of the coffeemaker.

"What?" he choked, afraid he had misheard. Certain she hadn't said what he thought she had.

She turned to face him, pressing her bottom back against the counter. She looked so distant. So far away from him. So somber. "Another woman. Is there one?"

He blinked, just to make sure he still could. Her

question, and the implications of it, were so bizarre as to be impossible. "You're serious, aren't you?"

She nodded slowly, then tucked her chin into her chest and studied the towel she grasped in her hands.

He began shaking his head. "Oh, no, Jolie. There isn't another woman." How could there be? She'd filled his heart and his life so completely there hadn't been room for anyone else in his heart. Not even his own brother.

He cleared his throat. "I haven't even looked at anyone else other than you for more than seven years."

She briefly met his gaze, a ray of hope lighting her eyes even as she worried her bottom lip between her teeth. Then she dropped her gaze again, saying nothing.

He didn't know what he expected her response to be. Relief? Curiosity? A follow-up question? Maybe even something to indicate what had made her ask such a question. But she merely turned back toward the coffee-maker, as if it needed her full attention in order to brew.

Surely she knew that he'd loved her more than anything in the world? That he could never feel for anyone else what he had felt—and still felt—for her?

And surely she knew that all she had to do was say six simple words and they could have it all back again: *I quit the fire station, Dusty.*

Jolie's heart pounded thickly in her chest as she gripped the edge of the counter and clamped her eyes shut. She wanted so much to believe Dusty. But somehow it was easier for her to think that someone else had come between them. A nameless, faceless someone much more beautiful than she, someone with whom she couldn't hope to compete. Someone on whom to pin the blame for the distance that separated them like the Great Lakes combined to create a gaping gulf. Yes, the mere prospect of another woman being the object of Dusty's attention, being the recipient of his hot touch, having permission to kiss his generous mouth, twisted her stomach into knots. But the truth that she might be to blame for what had happened to them...well, that cut even deeper, harsher, the pain a physical burning that threatened to turn her inside out.

Overly aware of his gaze on her, probing her, she forced herself to move. To busy herself. Prevent herself from responding to that gob-smacked expression on his too handsome face. Anything to stop herself from stepping toward him and gently easing the confused wrinkles from his forehead, running the pad of her thumb over his bottom lip. She opened the oven door and checked the meat loaf she'd put in earlier, though her mind lagged a split second behind her actions and it took her a moment to register what she was doing. Finally, she gauged the loaf done and placed the pan on the stovetop, then turned down the heat and placed a foil-wrapped baguette in to warm.

She knew Dusty had moved to stand next to her without having to see his tall frame from the corner of her eye as he took the hand mixer out of the cabinet, then collected milk and butter from the refrigerator to make the mashed potatoes. Just like he always had.

As impossible as it seemed, Jolie swore she could feel his heat bridge the few feet separating them. It swept over her skin like a caress, urging her closer to the man it seemed she'd always loved. A man who no longer loved her, despite the passion-filled kiss they'd shared that morning. The truth was, if he loved her, he'd never have left her.

They moved around the kitchen like two ghosts, performing tasks they had hundreds of times before. But while their actions reflected their past familiarity, the differences loomed between them like so many unspoken words. Words that crowded her throat now, choking her, and making her feel bound by yards of rope though she moved freely.

As if through silent agreement, finally they sat down at the table, dinner covering the surface. Jolie felt as if she might jump out of her skin at any moment, the suspense of Dusty's silence eating away at her quiet resolve to get through the meal without saying anything that might reveal how hurt she was. Expose how thickly her heart beat in her chest just being this near to him. Show him how much she wanted to explore all the explosive emotions his kiss had reawakened that morning.

"Is that what you really thought, Jolie?" Dusty asked quietly, pushing away his plate. "That there was…that I was…involved with another woman?"

She looked at him and she recognized the move for the mistake it was the instant she made it. He was hard enough to handle from across the room. In fact there was a time when she didn't think the town of Old Orchard large enough to keep her away from him. But up this close, just an arm's length away, he was devastatingly tempting. The rich Irish-coffee brown of his eyes, the strong shape of his jaw, the fresh, warm smell of his skin combined to make her stomach drop to somewhere in the vicinity of her feet.

Her heart skipped a beat. Her palms dampened. And her stomach tightened in acute awareness. Her body betrayed her as surely as he had.

She gave a wry smile. "Like, do you mean had I found any lipstick on your collar, any unexplained phone numbers on our bill?" Her attempt at humor fell well short of the mark, making her even more tense. "No," she said, forcing her gaze away. "No, I didn't really think there was someone else." She bit her bottom lip as she collected their plates. "Even if there were... well, it wouldn't matter, would it?"

Her gaze caught on the white of the divorce papers still sitting facedown on the corner of the table and her throat closed.

He caught her arm when she would have dived for the sink, anywhere that required her to be at least a room's length away from him. The mere feel of his skin against hers chased the breath from her lungs.

"But it does matter, Jolie. Or else you wouldn't have asked."

Jolie knew she should tug her arm from his. Walk away as though her entire body weren't clamoring for his touch. Pretend she didn't care one way or another if he'd been with someone else since he'd left her six months ago. But the truth was, she did care. Not a night went by that she didn't long for him to be next to her in that big bed they'd picked out at the weekly flea market on Route 108. That she didn't squeeze her thighs tightly together, needing him with an intensity that scared her.

That she wasn't forced to shove away her tears when she thought that at that very moment he might be sharing his heat with someone else.

It was during those moments that she felt more alone than she ever had. Even after her parents had perished in that fire when she was six. Even in the days after Dusty had left and she'd existed in a befuddled haze, completely incapable of grasping the new reality.

Just having him in the house, back in town, made her feel somehow alive again. Made her recognize that she'd been little more than half a person since he'd gone. And ignited a craving in her that set her body on fire.

The plates clattered back to the table and she twisted her arm until she was grasping his forearm just as he was grasping hers. She met his gaze, not encouraged by the wary shadow in his eyes, but not repelled by it, either. She thought of their scorching kiss that morning. Wondered if he'd really wanted her as much as she'd wanted him. Or whether her imagination had cooked up his reaction, made her see things that she wished were true but really weren't there.

But most of all she felt the overwhelming desire not to be alone.

He made a sound low in his throat then tugged her closer, until she was faced with the decision to either pull away or topple into his lap. She chose the latter, gripping his steely shoulders to anchor herself as her hair briefly swept between them then swayed away.

He brushed his mouth against hers. Jolie's breath snagged in her throat.

"It's been so long since I've wanted anyone but you,

Jolie, I wouldn't even recognize attraction to another woman," he murmured against her cheek.

She let her eyes flutter closed, drinking in his words, absorbing them, storing them away for some undefined time in the future when she might need them. When the loneliness grew unbearable. So she could dust them off and pull them back out, remember that at one time the man she loved had once loved her, too.

Dusty was watching her too closely, too intensely, and she dropped her gaze to his chest. He caught her chin and forced her gaze to his again.

"Damn, woman, but you confuse the living hell out of me."

She opened her mouth to respond, but he trapped the words inside with his own mouth, claiming her lips with fevered intensity. Rendering her incapable of doing anything but receiving his hungry attentions.

His hand dropped from her chin to her neck. She was afraid that he could feel the rapid beat of her pulse there, beneath her too hot skin. He slanted his mouth the other way, and she dragged in a deep breath, then launched an assault on his mouth that equaled the power of his. She boldly stroked his tongue with hers and hungrily pulled at his lips, relearning the taste of him. The feel.

He groaned and threaded his fingers through her hair.

Suddenly sitting across his lap wasn't enough for Jolie. A ravenous, seemingly insatiable need to be closer yet consumed her. Keeping contact with his mouth, she awkwardly stood, then repositioned her legs and strad-dled him, not stopping until the juncture of her thighs rested solidly against the growing ridge in his jeans.

"Oh, how I've missed you, Dusty," she whispered, knowing somewhere deep in her mind that she shouldn't have said the words but helpless to stop herself.

She tugged mindfully away, feeling suddenly bare… exposed…all too vulnerable.

But when she looked into his eyes, she saw exactly what she needed to see. Instead of wariness, she saw understanding. Rather than doubt, she saw compassion. In the place of indifference, she saw sheer passion.

He tugged her mouth back down to his, slipping his hot tongue between her teeth and tangling it with hers. She moaned and melted against him again, uncaring of what she'd revealed. Right now, this moment, this is what she wanted…what she needed.

Just when she thought she couldn't surpass the dizzying heights merely kissing him induced, Dusty dropped a palm to her breast and squeezed the aching mound of flesh through the fabric of her sweater, and the pleasure principle heightened within her.

"Tell me…what have you missed, Jolie?" he asked huskily, following the material of her sweater down to the hem, then trailing his fingers underneath. She shivered as he spanned her rib cage, then slipped his fingers under her bra and freed her left breast. "Did you miss this?" He feathered his thumb over the hard peak, sending a jolt of hot, searing heat straight to her stomach.

She moaned and increased the tempo of her kiss, pulling his tongue deep into her mouth, running her own along the uneven ridge of his teeth, feeling as if she wanted to swallow him whole.

The pressure of his fingers against the vee of her

jeans nearly sent her leaping out of them. He easily found her trembling core through the thick material and pressed inward. "Or did you miss this?"

She shuddered so violently she had to drag her mouth from his and grasp his shoulders to keep from sliding to the floor and dissolving into a puddle of unsatisfied lust.

His groan sounded against her ear, then he drew the tip of his tongue down the sensitive shell. "It's been so very long. Too long."

His vehement yet somehow reluctantly said words proved a catalyst, pushing her to the edge then over. Her muscles contracted and convulsed. She automatically clung to him, riding out the brief, delicious series of spasms even as he coaxed them further by making gentle circles around her throbbing womanhood through the denim of her jeans.

Finally, she rested the temple of her forehead against his, her eyes closed, her lips parted as she drew in gulping breaths of air.

Her position listing against him caused him to move his hand to her hip and he followed with his other hand on her other hip until he gripped her firmly, pressing her further against the hard ridge of his arousal. Her breath caught.

"Is that what you missed, Jolie?" he rasped.

She drew slowly back, holding his gaze with hers, all too willingly tumbling into the deep brown depths of his eyes. She reached between them, drawing her fingers along the length of him, then squeezing his erection through the thick denim. "This…is what I missed."

That wasn't entirely true. She'd missed everything. The sound of him in the shower, the scent of his shaving cream every morning. She missed the rustling of the newspaper as he read every last word over breakfast, and the way he gulped his orange juice down in one long sip. She'd even missed the way he left his shoes sprawled across the entry hall so that she tripped over them every time she came through the door.

She restlessly licked her lips. But most of all, she missed the way he used to love her. Unconditionally. Unabashedly. Shamelessly.

She missed *them*.

For a long moment she couldn't breathe. She merely sat and stared at him, her heart thundering in her chest. Her throat tight with emotion and longing. He returned her gaze. As if he understood as well as she did that they were facing a momentous decision in that instant. Whether to take things further…or to stop right where they were.

Chapter 5

Dusty watched the way Jolie ran her pink tongue along the soft, swollen flesh of her lips and knew that the decision, no matter how weighty, had been effectively lifted from his hands.

No matter the consequences, he wanted Jolie. The woman who was still his wife. *Now.* And that nothing short of the house being on fire would stop him from taking her.

He felt the jutting of her hipbones under his fingers and strengthened his grip. She made a soft sound of protest deep in her throat. Leaning forward, he claimed her mouth even more possessively, drinking from her sweetness like a man starved for her taste.

Six long, empty months separated now from the last

time he'd sunk into Jolie's hot flesh. Roughly one hundred and eighty nights when he'd rolled over looking to hold her, press himself against her, only to find her not there. And living with the knowledge that he had been the one who had been forced to leave had been sheer torture. Even toward the last days of their marriage, as the distance between them grew greater, they'd always come together at the end of the day, when the lights were out, their limbs entwined, their love-making sacred territory neither one of them was willing to sacrifice.

Now he pressed himself against her and groaned. While he may have wickedly teased her with his words, all along he knew he'd been the one who had missed this…wordless coming together. This joining of him with Jolie that defied explanation and rationale. When they were together this way, the world looked different. He felt different. And the night before he'd left, he'd been afraid he'd never feel that way again.

Apparently sensing the shift in his demeanor, Jolie fervently kissed him back, leaning back to allow him to tug off her sweater, then making the movements needed in order for him to strip off her jeans and panties.

He visually devoured every precious inch of flesh he exposed, noticing the deepened hollows, the more pro-nounced ridge of her ribs. He noted yesterday that she had lost weight, but didn't realize until this moment just how much. He pressed his mouth against the flesh between her breasts and closed his eyes, wondering what other changes the past six months had wrought on her. Whether the scar from the third-degree burn he

knew covered her back from shoulder blade to hipbone
had lessened.

He didn't get a chance to pursue the train of thought
for long. Jolie was tugging and pulling at the waist of
his jeans, freeing him, then taking the straining length
in her hot palms. Caressing him in that way that had
always driven him crazy with need.

He grasped her hips and pulled her to straddle him
once again, his gaze plastered to her heaving breasts,
high and pert and hard, in perfect proportion with her
narrow waist and curvy bottom. The tip of his erection
rested against her moist entrance. He knew a moment
of caution. They had never used protection. Not when
they'd first made love, because their coming together
had been hot and heavy and the thought of scrambling
for a condom had never crossed his mind. And the topic
of condoms had never been broached after they got
married and they had wanted to get pregnant immediately. They hadn't used them once in the five years they
were married.

Should they use protection now?

He groaned. Even if the answer was yes, he didn't
have anything on him.

He watched her closed eyes, knowing she was completely oblivious to his dilemma, as she gripped his
shoulders. Catching her bottom lip between her teeth,
she pressed against his erection, then her slick, hot flesh
was sliding down over him, ripping the conflict straight
from Dusty's mind.

Every last one of his muscles tensed as he strained
up against her. She was so gloriously tight. So slick. So

wonderfully warm and inviting. And he was so hungry for her he could have cried out.

Clutching her hips, he guided her away, then down again, amazed by the myriad sensations pumping through his body. From the heart-pounding surge of his blood, to the heat covering his skin from neck to toe. His gaze was fastened on Jolie's face…the way she pulled shallow breaths between her parted lips…the shadow of her lashes against her flushed cheeks….

He thrust upward, filling her completely. But he yearned for more than her physical closeness. He wanted to know she was there with him fully… completely.

"Open your eyes for me, Jolie," he asked raggedly.

He watched her close her eyelids even tighter, then drew her against him, reveling in the feel of her silken hot skin against his. She shivered as he dragged his fingers over her right breast and squeezed.

"Please," he murmured.

She ground against him and he groaned.

Finally, her eyelids cracked open and she gazed at him. Her blue eyes were nearly black with growing need as she tilted her hips forward, taking him in even deeper. He gripped her tightly, holding her still before he toppled over the edge he was perched on. Only when she began to murmur in protest did he plunge into her again. Then again. And again. He ran his fingers over her right breast, pausing to pinch the swollen peak, then dragged his fingertips down her stomach, holding her still as he plunged again.

Her hair lay against her skin like silk; her eyes were filled with passion and half-lidded; her pink, swollen lips parted as she made soft panting sounds. She was more beautiful than she'd ever been at that moment. Her every emotion displayed on her face for him to see.

She'd been distant from him for so long, he knew what her exposing herself to him now was costing her. And he was glad for it.

He withdrew from her, gritting his teeth with the effort it took not to ram into her like nobody's business, make up for the six months they'd been apart in no time flat. But he knew she'd always liked to take things slow. That despite her brief climax earlier, he needed to stroke Jolie just right, touch her just so, to make her blow apart. And that watching her do so was more powerful, sexier, than even his own climax.

He leaned into her, drawing a hardened nipple between his lips and nibbling on it. Then he pulled it into his mouth, rolling his tongue around the pale crest, before drawing her in deeper. She whimpered softly and arched against his mouth, grinding her pelvis needfully against his.

He dragged his tongue along her silken skin to her other breast, then laved that one with the same attention, suckling her until she made catlike mewling sounds and was clutching desperately at his shoulders, begging for him to continue his lovemaking.

His blood roaring past his ears, he slipped his hands under her knees, then slid them up to support her lush bottom, holding her slightly aloft from him. Then he thrust hard upward, the position allowing him to go deeper and harder. Jolie cried out and her muscles contracted around him, drawing him in. He thrust into her again…then again…then again. Until she called out his name and stiffened in climax.

Dusty braced himself to watch her. To drink in every wondrous shudder of her body. Watch the way her breasts shivered. The oval of her mouth as she cried out. But his own climax was too close…and ultimately too much for him to control. He finally allowed himself to tumble into that undulating inferno of bright color right after her.

He dragged in thick gulps of air, his temple resting against hers, the thundering of his heartbeat pumping against hers. He drew his fingers down along her side, drinking in her shiver. Then he circled around to her back, feeling the sandpapery rough stretch of skin there. The burn that had nearly taken her life along with his brother's.

"Jolie?"

Her muscles stiffened and soon she was pushing at his shoulders. Dusty resisted, needing to touch the area that had caused them both so much pain.

Then he realized it hadn't been him who'd said her name. Rather someone else had. Someone who had come in through the front door. A woman. It dawned on him that Jolie wasn't trying to twist away from him because he was touching her burn scar. She was trying to save them both from a potentially very embarrassing moment.

Cursing under his breath, Dusty pulled away from her. The silence in the house was deceptive, and they both knew not to trust it. They'd lived in the town too long for that. They scrambled for the cover of the laundry room just off the kitchen with what Dusty hoped was all their clothes. While he hadn't taken anything off,

Jolie was stripped of every last scrap of clothing. It took Herculean effort not to watch her as she struggled into her panties and jeans, then bra and sweater.

"Jolie?" came the woman's voice again.

Damn small towns, Dusty thought. He couldn't remember a time when they'd locked their doors. Everyone's house was open to everyone else. And while midnight visits weren't considered proper protocol, early evening drop-bys were perfectly acceptable. And one of their neighbors had definitely just dropped in for a visit.

"Wait."

Dusty grasped Jolie's wrist where she'd been about to leave the tiny laundry room. He caught his breath at the traces of passion still visible in her deep blue eyes, along with a boatload of confusion. He ignored both and reached up to smooth the thick tangle of her light brown hair. She caught on and managed to complete the finger-combing and shape it neatly into place. Then she reached out and ran her fingers along his upper lip, where his mustache used to be.

Dusty tucked a stray strand of hair behind her ear, then swallowed thickly. "Jolie, I…"

He what? What could he possibly say at a time like this? We'll continue this later? I had a great time, but I'm sorry, I really didn't mean for that to happen? Or how about, Bad habits are hard to break?

It turned out he didn't have to say anything, for Jolie must have been thinking the same thing. That the rip in time they'd just created out there on the kitchen chair was a mistake. He saw it there on her flushed face. In the wrinkle between her brows.

"I know," she said quietly, then pulled gently away from him and went into the kitchen.

Jolie tried to brace herself for seeing the unexpected visitor. Used whatever strength hadn't been drained out of her to rein in the emotions pulsing thickly through her veins with every beat of her heart. Attempted to arrange her face into some sort of neutral mask that would hide what had just happened between her and Dusty. But the moment she spotted her sister-in-law, Darby Conrad, standing in the kitchen doorway taking in the abandoned dinner dishes and two place settings on the table, all she wanted to do was throw herself into her best friend's arms and sob out all her troubles.

If Dusty wasn't a few feet away, she might have done just that. If Darby didn't have a whole host of troubles of her own, she definitely would have. But since neither was the case, she took in a quiet breath and smiled.

"Well, look who the cat dragged in."

Darby raised her gaze and returned her smile. "If that's a comment on what I look like, I take offense. I'd like to think that since today is the first time I've put on makeup in…well, months, that I look a little better than a soggy play toy. Or worse, a dead field mouse."

Jolie tightly hugged the pretty brunette, then laughed nervously and avoided Darby's gaze as she pulled away. "You always look great."

Which was exactly the wrong thing to say and she knew it the instant the words were out. Ever since Erick died, she seemed inexplicably sensitive about her appearance.

But being the trouper she was, Darby easily glossed over the gaffe and began chatting about everything and nothing while Jolie collected the dinner dishes and put them in the sink. All the while she quaked inside, her sex swollen and throbbing from Dusty's possessive attention, her lips raw and sensitive from his kisses, and her mind swirling alternately with questions and answers.

Why? was the one that emerged most frequently.

Why had Dusty come home?

Why had Dusty kissed her?

Why had Dusty made love to her?

Why hadn't he come out of the laundry room yet?

"What's this?"

Not much got past Darby. And now wasn't going to prove the exception. Jolie looked over her shoulder to where Darby was picking up a sheaf of papers from the floor. *The divorce papers.* Her pulse leaping, she nearly sprinted the short distance between them and impolitely snatched the papers from her soon-to-be ex-sister-in-law's hands. "Oh, nothing. Just some things concerning the house that the Realtor wanted. Boring stuff."

Darby's frown was all-too-telling. And the shift from frown to grin was head-spinning as Darby's attention moved beyond probing Jolie's face for answers to an undetermined spot somewhere over her shoulder.

"Dusty!" Darby cried, practically catapulting herself into his arms.

Jolie glanced away from his questioning gaze and his more-than-a-little gob-smacked expression.

"Oh, God! When did you get in? Why didn't you tell

me you were coming to town when we spoke the other day? It's been forever."

Darby's rapid-fire, enthusiastic questions filled the silence that loomed between Jolie and Dusty. Jolie was almost glad for it. Almost.

Dusty had called Darby? The other day? Had he kept in touch with his brother's widow? Apparently he had. And a part of her was glad that he'd stayed connected to some part of his family. Still, that didn't stop the knife-sharp pain that sliced through her chest at the knowledge that he hadn't called her once in the past six months. All communication had come through his attorney. Initially, she had talked directly to his lawyer. Then she'd decided the task was too painful and had hired old Tom Handland in town to handle the communications.

She hadn't even known where Dusty was, beyond the city. Didn't even have his phone number should she have needed to contact him. Wanted to hear his voice. Ask him the question that stole sleep from her at night.

Yet he'd been in touch with Darby.

Darby linked her arm through Dusty's and led him toward the table. Jolie realized she had the divorce papers twisted tightly in her hands and smoothed them out and dropped them facedown onto an empty chair.

"Jolie, why didn't you tell me he was coming?" Darby asked.

Because I didn't know. But she didn't say the words. Instead, she smiled. "Do you want some coffee?"

Darby hummed. "I'd love some."

Jolie didn't ask Dusty if he'd like a cup. She automatically pulled three cups out of the cabinet and poured the fresh-brewed coffee into each.

"My mom's watching the kids," Darby was telling Dusty as Jolie put the cups on the table and moved theirs to sit in front of them. "I didn't think it was a good idea to bring them into town to go shopping for Halloween costumes. You know kids. They're adamant about being ghosts...until they see the pumpkin costumes." She looked at where Jolie sat across from them. "Oh, and I can't thank you enough for bringing by that game of Candyland yesterday, Jolie. The twins love it. Oh, excuse me. They've informed me that they don't like to be referred to as 'the twins.' Anyway, it was all I could do to get Erin and Lindy into bed last night. And even then they insisted on sleeping with the game on the floor between their beds. Don't let on, but I know they snuck in a couple plays after lights out."

Jolie waved her away, trying to pretend she was following the conversation, even participating in it, though she felt as if she were viewing the table from ten feet above it. "I'm glad they like it."

She blinked her gaze up from her coffee, realizing she hadn't heard Dusty say anything since coming out of the laundry room. She thought maybe he was as confused as she by what had happened between them and needed a few minutes to gather his thoughts. Instead, she was surprised to see his face pale, his hands tight against his cup though he had yet to drink from it, and his eyes wide and unseeing.

It occurred to her that this was the first time he'd seen

his sister-in-law since his brother Erick had died six months ago.

Her stomach twisted into a tight knot.

Darby took a long pull from the coffee. "Oh, you don't know what a treat this is. I think giving up coffee was one of the hardest things to do when I was pregnant. And, well, of course now I wouldn't dare drink it regularly. Erin and Lindy try my nerves enough."

Slowly, Darby's voice began to fade and she, too, stared down into her coffee cup as though looking for answers in the murky depths.

Jolie told herself her sister-in-law had it much worse than she did. After six years of marriage, two beautiful twin girls, and building up a ranch together, Darby had lost her husband. Permanently. No father for her children. No husband for her. He hadn't just moved to another town hours away. He'd…died.

With her and Dusty… Well, given what had just happened between them at this very kitchen table, she wondered if things would ever really be over between them. There remained a link between them that no divorce papers could hope to sever.

Was that how she was destined to live out her life? Waiting for Dusty to walk back through that door? Hope for a few stolen moments here and there when their paths crossed? Is that all there was?

No. She'd asked herself those same questions weeks ago and had come to the conclusion that she couldn't do that. Couldn't live that way. She had to forge a path for herself alone. Without Dusty. And that included the selling of this house.

Jolie looked up to find Darby watching both her and Dusty curiously. "So…" she said slowly. "What was going on between the two of you when I came in, anyway? Did I interrupt something?"

Dusty pushed from the table so abruptly, that same panicky expression on his face, that Jolie started and Darby's brows furrowed in concern.

"I'm…sorry. I just remembered something I have to do," he said.

He started for the door then hesitated, his gaze raking Jolie's burning face, then falling on Darby. Jolie could have sworn she saw guilt in the depths of his brown eyes. But there wasn't anything for him to feel guilty about. Was there?

"It was good to see you, Darby. I'm glad you and the girls are doing so well."

With that, he stalked from the room, the closing of the door moments later announcing that he'd left the house entirely.

Silence reigned for long minutes as the two women considered his hasty departure. Jolie stared after the empty space that had been filled with Dusty's considerable presence, pondering his odd behavior. He had looked as if it had been torture being in the same room with Darby. But why? He and his sister-in-law had always gotten along well.

"Well," Darby said, finally breaking the silence. "What was that about? Is…is something happening between the two of you?"

Too much…yet so little, Jolie thought, shivering as she remembered his probing, skillful touch, and the distance in his eyes when she'd first seen him standing in the doorway. "Sorry," she said quietly, turning her gaze on Darby. "I don't know what's wrong."

"Maybe you don't, but I think I do," Darby said. "He just did what he does on the phone when he calls once a week. He asks me how the girls and I are, asks whether we need any money, then he hangs up with hardly a goodbye."

Jolie shook her head, still not understanding.

"Don't you see? He thinks he's the one responsible for Erick's death. It took me a while to figure it out. Survivor's guilt. I read up on it once, you know, for myself. Anyway, his avoidance of anyone connected to Erick is a classic sign."

Jolie felt as if she'd been run over by a bulldozer going full speed.

She'd never looked at the situation quite like that. Yes, Dusty had understandably been overwhelmed by the loss of his brother. But the anguish in his eyes just now was even deeper than it had been the day Erick had died. Had she been so concentrated on their own problems she hadn't been able to look beyond them to him? To what motivated him? To what had wormed its way deep into his heart, making him do what he had?

Her heart contracted painfully and it took everything she had not to get up and go after him.

The following morning, Dusty pounded away at installing new subflooring in the master bath, his muscles aching, his mind mercifully devoid of thought.

This trip back home—back to Old Orchard—wasn't

turning out to be anything like he'd hoped it would be. First there had been his hot reaction to seeing Jolie again after he'd thought he'd chased her out of his heart. A reaction that had led to them making love on the kitchen chair. Then he had seen Darby again after so long.

What did a man say to a woman whose husband was dead…because of him?

His muscles bunched and he pounded harder, determined to stop the thought in its tracks.

Six months had passed since he'd lost Erick in that fire. Six long, torturous months in which he'd wake up in the middle of the night covered in a cold sweat, imagining flames licking around the edges of his bedroom and calling out his brother's name.

From the word go Dusty had felt something wasn't right that night. An odd sort of foreboding had shadowed him throughout dinner at the station, and an emergency run out to the Clemens place, where one of their boys had managed to feed a toe to the lawnmower. He'd tried to shake it off, debated whether or not to share his thoughts with Erick, but ultimately kept quiet about them, seeing as there was only an hour to go on their shift.

"Pop quiz, hotshot," Erick had called out, leading the way up the emergency exit steps in the ten-story medical office building perched on the edge of town. "If paper's flash point is 451 degrees, how hot does it need to be for a sock to burn?"

Dusty remembered the sound of their quick, booted footsteps echoing through the stairwell as he pulled the attack hose behind him. The fire was called in by the night watchman and was said to be isolated on the sixth floor, though no site inspection had been made. "Let me guess. You've been assigned to another stint at the academy, huh?"

Erick had made a sound like a buzzer, indicating a wrong answer. "Six hundred degrees Fahrenheit." He stopped outside the door to the sixth floor, checking the metal for heat, then opened it. "And yeah, I'm scheduled for the next set of rookies in two weeks."

With each step Dusty took down the stylishly decorated hall, the sense of danger he'd experienced all day spiked even higher. He looked sharply around, feeling as if someone was following him. The situation was proving to be one of those where you knew there was a fire, you could smell the fire, you just couldn't see the damn fire.

Erick continued on ahead, checking, then opening doors on either side of the hall as he went. "Question number two," he said, peeking inside another office, then crossing the hall. "What do you get when—"

He reached for the door handle without checking the exterior for heat and Dusty's heart had surged up into his throat. "Back draft!" he shouted the instant Erick turned the handle. The door bowed ominously inward, then before Erick could turn his head toward the barrier, it exploded outward, slamming into his brother head-on, a rolling cloud of flame completely engulfing him.

Dusty's vision slowly returned to the here and now, to the silent and secure bathroom surrounding him. He'd never forget that night for as long as he lived. The night the fire had roared from behind that door, wild, hungry, out of control, and claimed his brother's life. He'd grown up knowing the ferociousness of that living, breathing animal called fire. Had been humbled by it as others were burned. Had been excited with the prospect of facing it when the call came in. But he'd never expected to sacrifice his brother to the red monster.

In one horrifying moment, Erick was gone, and Dusty was at risk of losing Jolie, as well, as she hovered on the other side of the fire on the perimeter of the building and fell victim to the same explosion. He'd experienced a fear so acute he'd thought his heart might explode. What he'd believed had been courage, bravery, he'd discovered was nothing but foolish ignorance.

So he'd quit the department and begged Jolie to resign, as well.

But she'd not only stubbornly rejected the idea, she refused to even consider it. To weigh how important it was to him that she stop putting herself at risk every single hour of every day. Instead, as she'd lain in the hospital bed, she had looked at him as though he was crazy, even though half her back was covered with third-degree burns. Her face was unnaturally pale against the white linen, and her blue eyes threw flames not unlike the ones that had burned her. And threatened to burn him.

Dusty let the hammer fall to his side, then dropped his chin to his chest. His eyes were full of grit from where he'd been so concentrated on the task of installing the flooring.

He couldn't do it again. Attend the funeral of another loved one. Especially when that loved one made a point of repeatedly placing her life in danger. He didn't think he could survive it. Not this time.

Angry at his own weakness, he pushed from the floor

and made his way back downstairs. When he'd left Darby and Jolie alone last night, he'd spent hours walking the town streets, then when he couldn't take even one more hearty welcome-back, when he had no intention of staying, he headed out of town, on the old town road, walking until he couldn't walk anymore. He'd hitched a ride back with one of the Jansen brothers somewhere around midnight.

Jolie had been fast asleep. Or so she would have had him think. A wish he had decided to support. He hadn't wanted to talk to her just then. Didn't want to see that smear of pained confusion in her eyes that had been there after they'd made love earlier…and when he'd left her and Darby, feeling as though he might burst with the guilt that filled him.

He'd slept on the sofa. Or did what Jolie had been doing curled up in the bed upstairs—pretended to sleep. And continued to do so even when he'd heard her get up at seven, readying herself for her next twenty-four-hour shift at the fire station. It wasn't until sometime after the door had closed behind her that he'd gotten up, filled a cup with the strong coffee that she'd left for him, and headed straight upstairs to finish what he should have long ago.

Now, as he headed downstairs for the first time in five hours, he remembered that he hadn't thought to look for the divorce papers last night when he'd returned to the house. To check whether or not she'd signed them yet. But he did so now.

They weren't on the kitchen table where she had been reading through them the day before. They weren't in the desk drawer in the cluttered office they once shared. Nor were they anywhere in the living room or dining room. It wasn't until he'd basically given up the hunt, deciding that she must have taken them with her and in the middle of making himself a sandwich for lunch, that he found the folded papers in the silverware drawer.

Dusty forgot about the butter knife he'd been in search of and slowly took the papers out. Why had she put them there? He smoothed them out next to his makeshift hero sandwich and stared down at the top page. Conrad v. Conrad. The words made him shudder in disgust.

Since his return two days ago, very little about their predicament had seemed real somehow. But just reading the words brought everything back into focus. He'd officially petitioned the courts to end his marriage to the only woman he'd ever loved. To finally sever the ties that had bound them for so long, but had threatened to choke him in the end.

He slowly turned the pages, reading them one by one. There was no mention of property division, except for a notation about equitable distribution. Aside from the house. Which he'd decided to give to Jolie once the divorce was final. He glanced around the old, familiar kitchen, remembering the Realtor's sign he'd found out front, and his own sense of anger at discovering she'd intended to sell it.

He'd somehow imagined Jolie living in the place forever. Growing old there. Perhaps remarrying and adopting the children they had been unable to have. Never once had he thought she'd sell the place.

And why not? Hadn't he been the one anxious to

push the past aside and start anew? At least she had stayed in town. He…couldn't. He'd had to leave. Old Orchard was full of too many painful reminders of what had once been. And what would never be again.

He closed his eyes and breathed in the lingering scent of toast and coffee and crisp autumn leaves and knew he had to do what he came here to do, and then leave. The continuation of his work on the master bathroom was a way of wasting time. He'd contract out and have Branson and his company see to the work that remained. It wasn't good for either him or Jolie for him to stay one minute longer than he had to. Because the fact was he would be going again…and this time he wouldn't be coming back.

Suddenly not hungry, Dusty tossed the makings of his sandwich away then closed the silverware drawer. Staring down at the unsigned papers, he folded them up and tucked them into the back pocket of his jeans. A half hour later he had cleaned up the tools he'd been using on the master bath, packed up his few items of clothing, then closed the front door after himself. A quick stop at the fire station, and he'd be on his way out of town in no time.

He climbed into his truck. But before he could close the door, the shrill sound of a siren pierced his eardrums. He jerked to stare at the crossroads two blocks down, instantly spotting the pumper from the station. A truck Jolie would be on.

Dusty's gut tied into knots and he broke out in a cold sweat. Would he ever be able to hear a siren again without seeing his brother's lifeless face? Without the image of Jolie on a stretcher, a paramedic trying adamantly to breathe life into her still lungs?

He slammed the door and jerkily turned the key, the images and his reaction to them enough to spur him into action.

Chapter 6

"Get that intake line hooked up! Now!" Chief Gary Jones shouted over the roar of water from the attack lines and fire.

Jolie leapt immediately into action as Sal strung the intake line from the hydrant on the corner of Orchard and Washington. She opened the hydrant connection to the pumper, her heart beating a million miles a minute. Her turnout gear weighed sixty-eight pounds, but after seven years with the fire department, she didn't pay attention to the extra weight anymore. It was just part of the scenery. No firefighter went anywhere without the essentials. And that included her fire-resistant boots, fluorescent-striped coat and helmet, along with her gloves and bunker pants, while her face mask and air cylinder were nearby and easily accessible should she

be called on to go inside. As it was, fellow firefighters
Martinez and Holden were on search-and-rescue
rotation now. She glanced at the house behind her. A
familiar house she'd visited dozens of times, along with
nearly every other house in the small town. A house that
belonged to Angela Johansen, whom she had just
spoken to at the general store just the day before. A
house that would be little more than ash in five minutes
flat if they couldn't bring the fire under control. A task
looking less and less likely with every passing minute.
And so far they'd been on the scene for fifteen.

"They're still in there!" a woman shouted. "Angela
and little Ellie are still in the house. Why doesn't
somebody get them out?"

Jolie shot a glance over her shoulder, her hand slipping
on the nozzle through her protective gloves. Her heart
leapt up into her throat as Mrs. O'Riley came rushing from
across the street, wildly waving her arms and ignoring
Sheriff John Sparks and one of his deputies as they tried
to stop her from rushing into the burning building.

Jolie frantically looked back at the one-story clap-
board house. Red-and-yellow flames lapped out of the
two broken front windows over the porch, and gray-and-
black smoke swirled up in angry eddies toward the cold,
cloudless sky.

"They've got two guys in there now, Mrs. O'Riley,"
John was telling the hysterical woman. "If anyone can
get them out, they can. You're not going to do anyone
any good if you get in the way."

Jolie forced herself to concentrate on the task at hand.
What if Martinez and Holden couldn't get to the young

family in time? Dread slunk thick and steely through her tense frame.

She hated these fires the most. Ninety-nine percent of the time, the fires they were called on to put out weren't serious. Contained grease fires. Somebody who hadn't taken the wind direction into consideration while burning leaves. The odd mishap with the family grill. Most often they were called on to aid in situations that didn't include fire at all, performing in a strictly EMS capacity. Or helping attend to other miscellaneous mishaps, like the chicken incident.

But this…this was definitely a real fire. And that it was happening in a house that she was not only very familiar with, but that looked so very similar to the one she had grown up in but that no longer existed, the one that had claimed her parents' lives…well, this type of fire made her heart pump doubly hard and her stomach lodge in her throat.

Jimmying the valve switch to open the hydrant connection, she checked the gauges, then switched open the discharge gates to allow pressurized water to flow from four discharge lines. "Hoses a go!" she shouted, giving a thumbs-up in case Jones couldn't hear her but could see her.

She finished her task and helped Sal run the additional hoses toward the inferno. Sal took the line from her and straddled it in order to take the full pressure of it with his legs. Within moments another heavy stream of water was focused on the open door Martinez and Holden had disappeared into moments ago.

"Hold up!" Jones shouted, waving his arms.

Both hoses were turned immediately away toward the windows as a figure appeared in the doorway. Jolie's heart nearly leapt straight from her chest as she noticed Martinez…and he was carrying a lifeless form over his right shoulder. He stumbled out onto the porch, then down to the grass, where he laid Angela Johansen's inert form on the ground in front of him.

The paramedics rushed forward as Martinez pushed his face mask off and dropped to his knees. Moments later, Holden came out empty-handed and knelt down next to him.

Tires eating the cement sounded behind Jolie. She ripped her gaze away from where the paramedics were inserting a breathing tube into Angela's trachea to find Jeff Johansen stumbling from his truck and rushing to his young wife's side. "Angela! Oh, dear Lord, Angela!"

"Get him back," Chief Jones commanded.

John Sparks grasped him by the arms when he threatened to get in the way of the paramedics. "Let them work, Jeff."

The expression on Jeff's face was that of a rabid animal as his wide eyes took in the scene surrounding him. Jolie found it impossible to pull in a breath as he finally came to the conclusion she had.

"Where's Ellie? Where's my little girl?" Jeff shouted over the roar of the water, fighting John's attempts to restrain him.

Holden shook his head. "We couldn't find her, Jeff."

Jolie's knees threatened to give out as the impact of the news hit her. She started toward Jeff, instinct telling her what he was about to do…what she would have done had she been in his position. But before she could go two steps, he jerked himself free from John's grasp and launched himself toward the front door and the fire inside, before anyone else could catch him.

Oh, God, no.

Sparks started after him, but the chief caught him around the waist. "Can't let you do that, Sheriff. Dammit, we should have stopped him from going in. I'm not letting you in there, too."

Jolie's gaze darted urgently to Holden and Martinez as they struggled to get to their feet to go after Jeff, but they were in no shape to go back into the house so soon after coming out of it. A quick assessing glance told Jolie that she and the chief were the only free ones. Without hesitating, she grabbed her mask and tank and began shrugging into them.

The chief laid a restraining hand on her shoulder. "Martinez and Holden can handle him, Jolie."

She steadily held his gaze. "And Ellie? If they're going after Jeff, who's going to continue the search for Ellie?"

"We'll find out what happened to her…"

After, he'd been about to say. They were the same words he'd uttered twenty years ago when her parents had perished in the fire at their house.

She pushed past him, barely noticing a familiar truck pulling to a stop a short way away. *Dusty.* She pulled the mask over her face and motioned for Sal to proceed her in with a lead hose.

* * *

Dusty leapt from the truck as if it was on fire rather than the house, his breath trapped in his lungs, the bitter, acrid smell of the fire permeating his nose. He immediately spotted Jolie and her combative stance as she stood in front of Chief Jones in full gear.

A quick look around the scene told him more than five minutes' worth of conversation with any of his former colleagues. There were civilians in the house. The fire wasn't under control yet. His gaze fastened to his soon-to-be ex-wife.

Jolie was going in.

Fear, swift and complete, twisted like a set of knives in his stomach. Acting on it, he sprinted across the front lawn and grasped the back of Jolie's collar before she could launch herself mask-first into the flames.

"You're not going in there."

She stared at him through the protective face mask, her eyes round and determined, her mouth pulled tight. "Get out of my way, Dusty."

His glance fell to the fire ax she held and the way she had her booted feet planted shoulder-length apart. "I'm not…I can't let you go in there."

An unnamable something flickered in her eyes. Confusion. Curiosity. Anger. Perhaps equal measures of all. Then she was staring at him again. "Let me go so I can do my job."

He began shaking his head and she moved her arm so that he was forced to release his grip. "Jolie, I—"

"No, Dusty. What you're feeling right now is strictly personal. And as far as I'm concerned, you gave up any right to personal when you walked away from our marriage." She leaned closer, her voice muffled through the mask. "This is neither the time nor the place for this conversation. Now, if you'll excuse me."

Dusty was pushed to decide between bodily stopping her from entering the house, in which case he had to accept the possibility that she might flatten him, and stepping aside.

When Sal brushed by him with the hose, the decision was made for him. He'd done all he could. Now all that was left for him was to pray that everything would be okay. That Jolie would go in the house…and come back out again. In one piece. Unharmed. And alive.

Jolie couldn't see a thing. The interior of the house was pitch-black and the smoke choking the hallways was thick and impenetrable. Sal passed her, keeping the water aimed at the ceiling to cool the air and creating a minirainstorm inside the hall. In a slow, progressive crouch, Jolie checked the passageway to make sure a small form wasn't hunkered down, rendered unconscious by the smoke. Nothing. Using the head of her fire ax, she pushed open doors already left ajar by Martinez and Holden, making quick rounds of the rooms snaking off the hallway. The first bedroom, the master, she guessed, yielded nothing. No Ellie hiding under the bed or in the closet, trembling and afraid for her life.

An image flashed behind Jolie's eyelids. An image of herself sitting in the middle of her bed, clutching her sheets, flames licking over the sides of the mattress, smoke billowing from everywhere, it seemed, making her room seem eerily unattached from reality. A parallel universe of sorts in which no one could break through and from which she couldn't hope to free herself.

The scarred flesh between her knee and shin seemed to burn as if injured anew as she blinked against the image and pressed on down the hallway. Ellie's room lay to the right. A small room, no larger than ten by ten, with white furniture and stuffed animals even now smoldering in the far corner, smoke rising up from between their manufactured ears. The smoke edged its way under her mask and filled her nostrils with its acrid smell. There were days when it seemed she'd never rid herself of the smell. Days when she felt the odor permeated every cell of her body, was a part of her, a part that would remain forever.

"Ellie!" she called, hating her limited vision and mobility with her mask and full uniform and making adjustments to it. She checked under the bed. Nothing. In the white plastic toy box. Nothing. In the tiny closet that held all sorts of tiny little dresses that would never be the same again. Nothing. Ellie, it seemed, had vanished into thin air.

She turned at the door and took one last look around, her gaze riveted to the middle of the bed. It had been stripped of comforter by the team before her. But the pillows at the head remained. Pillows that suddenly moved.

Jolie's heart thundered in her chest as she made her way back toward the bed. Dropping the ax to the floor, she grabbed one of the pillows by the corner and flung it across the room. Her actions unearthed a tiny, pale foot that instantly disappeared beneath the other pillow, leaving only a hint of a lacy hem behind. Emotion choked Jolie's throat as surely as the smoke as she snaked her arms around the pillow and the tiny, bony form beneath it, picking both up in one fell swoop.

Arms instantly came around her neck, holding tight.

"It's okay, sweetie…Ellie…it's okay. Everything's going to be all right." She pulled her mask free and fit it over Ellie's wide-eyed face, thankful that the pillows had shielded her from taking in too much smoke. "Breathe normally. There you go. You'll see…everything's going to be fine."

Her gaze snapped onto Ellie's and she knew in that moment that she was lying. Nothing would be fine in the little girl's life again. She'd lost her mother. And her father, who was in the house somewhere looking for her, would either be seriously injured or fall victim to the fire himself. Nothing would ever be fine in little Ellie's life again.

Her blood racing through her veins double time, she rushed for the door, screaming into her radio that she had the girl…she had Ellie. In fact, she had to force herself to loosen her grasp for fear of snapping the five-year-old in two, she was holding her so tight. But in this smoke, she knew that if she lost her grip, if Ellie slipped away from her, the chances of finding her again lay somewhere between zero and nil.

"Hold on to me, baby," she whispered, smoothing back Ellie's blond curls and noting the lines of soot caused by the tracks of her tears. "That's it. Hold on tight. And promise you won't ever let go."

* * *

"She's going to blow!" one of the men called from where he was ventilating the roof.

Dusty rushed forward automatically. "No!" He wasn't sure if he'd said the word aloud, or if it was lodged somewhere deep in his chest, alongside the same cry he'd shouted the day he'd lost his brother and thought he'd lost Jolie, as well.

Not again. No…no…no. It couldn't possibly happen again. The law of averages went against his losing two loved ones in one lifetime to violent deaths, much less within such a short time frame.

Jolie's still in there! his mind cried. He stalked first toward the house, staring at the flames growing larger and hearing the ominous creaks that foretold that it might fall in on itself any minute.

Martinez and Holden trudged out, Holden dragging an unconscious and charred Jeff Johansen after him. Immediately after, Sal came out, pulling the hose out after him.

Where's Jolie? Oh, God, where's Jolie?

Dusty's legs felt simultaneously like jelly and lead. He turned toward the truck and grabbed a jacket, then stormed the front of the house…just as the door opened and a cloud seemed to belch out Jolie in a puff of smoke and air, right into his arms. He stumbled backward against the weight, then knew to get her out of there as quickly as possible. He swept her up into his arms and glanced down into her soot-covered face. Where was her mask? Then he saw the bundle she clutched in her arms like a precious, priceless package.

He knew a relief so complete, so overwhelming, that

his extensive training was what carried his legs toward the edge of the front lawn and safety, away from where the paramedics were even now hoisting Ellie's father onto a gurney and into an ambulance. He laid Jolie and her load on a bed of freshly raked leaves, staring down into her eyes, which seemed even more vividly blue against the grit covering her face. Behind them a menacing whoosh sounded, followed by the sound of cracking wood. He didn't have to look to know that the house had just collapsed in on itself. And the heat against his back told him the fire had arced outward, then back in again.

All he could see was Jolie.

The little girl in her arms struggled. Jolie let loose a small, strangled cry, then quickly sat up, taking Ellie with her. Dusty helped her take the mask off her face even as paramedics rushed to them, reaching for Ellie although it seemed Jolie might not let go.

"Please…" Jolie coughed, her voice rough and smoke-filled. "Be gentle…with her."

The female paramedic nodded. "I will."

But Ellie wouldn't let go. Her thin arms grasping Jolie's neck tightly, she looked as if she might do what the smoke had been unsuccessful in doing and choke her.

Jolie's eyes filled with compassion as she eased the seemingly fragile arms from around her. "It's okay…I told you everything was going to be all right… remember?"

The little girl's eyes, large in her urchin face, stayed focused on Jolie as she nodded.

Jolie smiled tremulously as she smoothed back her tangled hair. Dusty knelt, mesmerized.

"You need to go with Dana now, okay? She needs to check you out. Make sure you're okay." The arms sought Jolie's neck again, but she gently caught them in her hands. "She won't hurt you. I promise. You believe me, don't you?"

Again, Ellie nodded, not having said anything since she was brought from the house.

The other paramedic started to check Jolie, but she waved him away. "Take care of the girl. Ellie needs you more than I do."

Dusty sought Jolie's gaze, and finally she turned his way. He didn't have to say anything. Neither did she. Everyone in the town knew the Johansens. And everyone would also soon know that Angela had perished in the fire that even now was completely claiming the house behind them. And that Jeff's chances for survival were dim.

Everyone also knew that neither Angela nor Jeff had any extended family.

Dusty searched Jolie's wide eyes, seeing in their murky depths hope mixed with pain and fear.

"Come on, sweetie," Jolie said calmly to the girl she still held. "We both have to go to the hospital now."

Finally, little Ellie let go of her neck, allowing the paramedic to take her to the second waiting ambulance. Dusty slowly reached out his hand toward Jolie. She stared at it, then him, the emotions he'd glimpsed just moments ago eclipsed by wariness and confusion. Then she slipped her glove off and placed her hand in his. He marveled at how small it seemed in his, as he always had. He'd always thought she should have hands larger than his. Limbs to match the size of her heart...determination...courage.

He realized he was staring and forced himself to easily lift her from where she still sat on the mound of leaves. She coughed, a dry, crackling sound that racked her entire body. He tucked her into the curve of his arm and led her toward the station rescue truck, glad when she didn't protest or otherwise shuck his attentions. And feeling more mixed-up than ever.

Where did things stand between him and Jolie? He'd been so certain that the love they once shared was gone. That he'd shored up his heart against her. But as every minute ticked by, he not only remembered all those little, tiny things that, when added up, had made him fall in love with her in the first place; he was finding new, fresh reasons to draw a deep breath and allow her very essence to saturate the very depth of him.

This wasn't supposed to happen. The divorce papers were stiff and unforgettable in his back pocket. But for now all he wanted to do was feel her weight tucked against his side. Her hand in his. And thank God she still walked the earth.

Chapter 7

Dusty hated hospitals. Had loathed them ever since he was seven and he and Erick had been left to visit with their great-aunt Wilma while their parents went out for coffee. Mom and Dad had only been gone fifteen minutes. And when they'd left, Aunt Wilma had seemed fine, her false teeth flashing white against her purplish lipstick, her silver curly wig hanging cockeyed as she spoke to him and Erick.

But five minutes into a game of Go Fish, Aunt Wilma's head had listed to the side, her rheumy eyes staring straight at him, and she had died.

Even thinking about the memory made Dusty shudder. To this day, he still didn't think Erick had had a clue what had happened. He'd thought, and Dusty had convinced him, that Wilma had been playing a joke. Only he knew that there had been nothing funny about it. Not even his parents caught on to what had happened. After figuring out that his old aunt had died, he'd pretended to be tired of playing cards and announced that he was going to the drinking fountain. Erick, of course, had trailed right behind him. As far as Mom and Dad knew, they had been the first ones to discover Wilma's passing when they returned to the room a short time later.

Of course, there were other reasons why he didn't like hospitals. As far as he was concerned, the cold buildings represented illness, death and all things that reminded him that he wasn't indestructible, after all.

Aunt Wilma aside, there had been few times when he'd actually been in a hospital. Even when Erick had died in the fire, he'd waited until his brother had been taken to Reece's Funeral Home to view the remains, having seen all he needed to on the site, though Erick hadn't been officially pronounced dead until arrival at the hospital. DOA. Dead on arrival. When in fact life had seeped from his body long before then.

The majority of the three times he'd been to the hospital had been because of Jolie….

He waited outside her room. Rather, he wore the tile down in the hospital hallway. He peeked around the corner into the large, open space that comprised the emergency room. In one curtained-off area little Ellie, seemingly in shock, sat with a pediatric nurse, impervious to the nurse's attempts to engage her in a game she'd brought and had spread out on the bed. The soot had been wiped from her tiny face, her hair had been combed, but in her eyes there was a sadness that reached out and virtually grabbed Dusty where he stood. And when she blinked those same eyes and looked at him through the glass, he feared he'd lose his stomach altogether. Especially when her expression didn't change one iota. She seemed not to see him at all. Or worse, didn't care one way or another who was on the other side of the door.

Dusty shifted his gaze to the other side of the curtain, catching a glimpse of Jolie's chestnut hair from where she sat with her back to him, her back left bare by the skimpy hospital gown, as Tucker O'Neill ran the stethoscope up one side of her defined spine and down the other side as Jolie inhaled and exhaled. The examination was pretty much par for the course when anyone at the station took in more smoke than they should. Except in his case. Dusty had absolutely refused to sit through more than a cursory exam at the rescue truck whenever the occasion arose. He smirked at his own cockiness, which seemed like a lifetime ago. And pretty much it was another lifetime ago. He was no longer that same person who would rush into a fire without protection. The man who could stand by and not only watch his wife enter the cauldron of flame, but encourage her to go right alongside him.

No, that person was a stranger to him now. When he heard a siren, long moments passed before he could even breathe again.

Tucker O'Neill came out of the room and closed the door after himself. Dusty shifted to allow him passage, though his gaze remained glued to Jolie's back, the sight strangely mesmerizing.

"You know I could have Sparks write you up for being a Peeping Tom," Tuck said matter-of-factly, writing something on his chart.

Dusty managed a ghost of a grin at the man who was equal to him in age, but otherwise different. And it was more than that Tuck was his physical opposite with his longish, always-in-disarray blond hair and green eyes. While Dusty had once preferred to seek his excitement on the job and had lived an otherwise sedate life, Tuck was a mild-mannered doctor by day and a thrill-seeker by night. From leaping out of airplanes, bungee-jumping off of platforms, and driving his '67 Shelby Mustang, on his off hours he lived as if there were no tomorrow. Of course he ignored everyone when they told him there probably wouldn't be a tomorrow for him unless he settled down. He also ignored the advice that a good woman might help him do that.

"Nothing wrong with a guy looking at his own wife," Dusty said.

Tuck lifted a skeptical brow. "So long as she still is."

Dusty averted his gaze. It was already clear that Jolie hadn't told anyone about their impending divorce. Had she changed tactics? Had she said something to Tuck? If so, why?

He decided to play it light, until he knew either way. "You know something I don't?"

Tucker grinned. "Actually, I think I should be the one asking that question. You and Jolie know something we don't." He shrugged. "Not that I'm saying we should know, but it would make things easier if we knew if it was okay to ask her about you when you're not around."

Dusty met his old friend's gaze. "You're asking the wrong person, Doc."

"I see."

Dusty rubbed the back of his neck so hard he feared he might rub the skin clean off. "I'm glad somebody does." He dropped his hand to his side then sighed. "So, what's the prognosis?"

Tuck snapped the chart he held shut, then tucked it under his arm. "On you and Jolie?"

Dusty squinted at him, keeping his cringe to himself. "On Jolie's health."

"Oh. She'll be fine. Healthwise. Some minor smoke inhalation and she has the lungs of a fifty-year-old chain-smoker, but hey, it's part of the job, right?"

"Right."

"Oh, and when you get a chance, remind her that this doesn't count as her annual physical. She's going to have to come in and go through the whole nine yards."

"I will." He glanced toward the isolation door to the side. "Any news on Jeff Johansen yet?"

"No, sorry, there's not. I'm just heading over there myself to see how I can help. I'll probably be in the way, but I feel like I should be doing something, you know?"

He nodded. Oh, did he know.

"Did you want to see her?"

Dusty hesitated, knowing Tuck was back to talking about Jolie again.

Yes, he wanted to see her. More than anything else

he could think of doing right that minute. But was it wise to see her?

Wise or not, he knew he had to. "Yeah. Is it all right if I go in?"

Tuck nodded. "Go on ahead."

Dusty started to.

"Oh, and Conrad?" He turned at the sound of Tuck's voice. "If you need anyone to talk to, you know, to vent on…I think my drinking arm's still in shape."

Dusty grinned, recalling that many had been the time when he'd taken off with Tucker O'Neill, John Sparks and Erick, climbed on top of the Clemens's hay silo, and knocked back a twelve-pack when they were teenagers. Often had also been the time when they'd puked their guts out over the side of that same silo. "I bet."

Tuck walked down the tiled hall, shaking his head and chuckling.

Dusty turned back toward the door. The nurse looking after Ellie had pulled the curtains surrounding her cubicle partially closed so he could no longer view the little girl and her haunted eyes. Instead, he headed for the other side of the curtain divider, distantly hearing the nurse's voice as she asked the little girl if she'd like to go down to the cafeteria to get something to eat, then asked, "Was that a 'yes'?" He guessed Ellie must have nodded, because he heard the shuffling of feet moments later as they left the room.

Dusty rounded the corner to find Jolie still with her back to him, tugging on her shirt. He stood rock still at the sight of the white flash of her bra and scarred skin, remaining silent until she'd finished buttoning up the front and started tucking the shirt in.

"You're doing it again," she said softly.

Dusty looked up and she slowly turned to face him. She must have washed up in the nearby bathroom, for there were no visible traces of the ordeal she'd gone through a mere half hour earlier. Aside from the smell. The odor wafted from Jolie as surely and more strongly than any perfume.

It was difficult to believe there had once been a time when he'd thought the scent of burning wood exciting.

"Doc O. gave me a thumbs-up."

Dusty nodded and tucked his thumbs into his front jeans pockets. "I know. I talked to him outside."

She passed him, reaching for her coat. Only as she draped it over her arm, he realized it wasn't her coat. It was his. His old denim coat, to be more precise. He lifted his gaze to hers, but she was already exiting the cubicle and peeking into the neighboring one.

"The nurse took her down the cafeteria."

She didn't say anything for a long moment, then asked, "Any word on Jeff?"

He shook his head. "You're not thinking about waiting around until some news comes through?"

She stood for a long moment, still looking blankly at the empty cubicle. Finally, she shook her head. "No."

She turned and headed for the door.

Dusty cleared his throat, catching the outer door when she opened it. "You want to get something to eat?"

She glanced at him over her shoulder. Petite shoulders that were held at a rigid, unyielding angle. "No. I should be getting back to the station." Then, in an after-thought, she quietly said, "Thanks."

"Don't mention it. Though I don't think your presence at the station would be welcome. Jones said for you to take the rest of the day off."

Her steps faltered. "Oh."

He smiled at her. "Yeah. Oh."

She averted her gaze, shifting the coat from one arm to the other where they stood in the middle of the bustling hallway. "I really should go, anyway."

Of course she would say that. Sometimes he thought Jolie would be lost if not for the fire station and her job. What would she do? Where would she go, if not for Jones and the crew, and the fires that needed dousing?

He ran his hand over his hair, then remembered the papers he had stuffed into the back pocket of his jeans. Papers that didn't seem so important now in light of what had happened in the past hour or so. His desire to hightail it out of town was replaced by the need to make sure Jolie was all right.

An idiot could recognize the similarities between what had happened at the Johansen place and the fire that had stolen Jolie's parents in the dead of night some twenty years ago. While she might be putting up a good front, he'd seen a heart-wrenching sorrow in her eyes when she'd sat on the Johansens' lawn, clutching little Ellie to her as if afraid that if she didn't, she might vanish into the air along with the suffocating, sky-choking smoke. He'd viewed that haunted expression in one other person's eyes: Ellie's just a few minutes ago.

As he followed Jolie from the hospital, he stridently

ignored that while he was forced to hurt her with their break-up, he would never do so at the cost of her emotional well-being. And one thing he knew for certain was that Jolie needed him right now. Needed him just as surely as she had twenty years ago as she clutched him, watching her parents' covered, still bodies being lifted from the only home she'd ever known.

He reached for his back pocket and shoved the papers a little more firmly down, then covered them with his jacket.

"Where are you going?" Jolie asked, once they were standing outside.

He shrugged, trying to appear indifferent. Only he'd forgotten for a moment who he was facing. Jolie knew him better than anyone and could see through any playacting. "I thought I'd swing by the station with you. You know, see if they could use any help."

Jolie's right brow nudged up a fraction of an inch.

He cleared his throat, then grinned. "Okay. So I know that Jones is going to send you home as soon as you show your face there. I thought maybe then you'd change your mind and catch lunch with me."

She nodded, this excuse making better sense to her apparently because she recognized it as the truth. At least a partial truth.

She shrugged into the jacket, his jacket, her cheeks touched with pink as she presumably noticed that it was his. "Okay. You win. Let me go by the station, just to make sure they don't need me, then I'll meet you at…"

He suspected she'd been about to say "home," then stopped herself.

"At the, um, house," she finished.

He nodded. "Tomato or clam?"

Her brows knit together.

"Soup. What kind do you want?"

The shadow of a smile tilted her lips even as she glanced down at her watch, then past him at the hospital doors, her mind, no doubt, on little Ellie and her father. "New England. I think there's a can in the pantry."

"Got it."

She turned to walk toward her Jeep, parked a short way away, his truck parked right next to it. She turned, walking backward. "I shouldn't be more than an hour."

"I'll give you half."

Her gaze darted away. "I have something else I want to see to first."

Dusty didn't like the sound of that, but was helpless to do more than watch her as she climbed behind the wheel of the Jeep and drove away.

Chapter 8

Jolie was distantly surprised she'd been able to make the forty-five-minute drive out to Hocking Hills Nursing Home, as badly frayed as her nerves were. But somehow she'd made it quicker than she would have thought possible. Now she sat staring at the colonial-style building set back against a stand of thick, autumn-painted trees, a large pond in front.

She didn't know what she'd hoped to accomplish by coming here. What she did know was that she'd willingly lied to Dusty for the first time in the forever that she'd known him. And that fact more than anything else bore out how very much the dynamics of their relationship had changed.

Then again, that she'd felt compelled to come out

here to visit her grandfather rather than talk things out with Dusty also spoke volumes.

Despite what she'd told him, she'd never intended to go back to the firehouse. She'd known that Jones wouldn't accept her presence there. It was par for the course for a firefighter to be sent home after an especially grueling run to recuperate, if only to get back in shape in time for the next run. Instead she'd driven way out here to talk to her grandfather.

She rubbed her fingertips against her closed eyelids, wishing she could have swung by the house for a quick shower and change of clothes before coming out. While she couldn't detect the odor on herself, she knew that others could from ten feet away. There was something about the smoke that made itself one with every fiber of clothing, clung to your skin and hair with such tenacity that sometimes she showered three times, scrubbing until her skin was raw and red, and she swore she could still smell the smoke.

She climbed from the Jeep and walked toward the entrance. Only after signing in and checking her grandfather's schedule did she climb up to the second floor to where his private room was down at the far end of the hall.

She rapped lightly on the thick, carved oak door, then stepped inside. Warm mid-afternoon light pooled in from the two curtained windows on either side of the neat bed, making the large room cozy and bright. Jolie smiled tremulously. "Hi, Gramps."

She gazed lovingly on his face, then shuffled awkwardly to a chair and sat down on the very edge. Everything at the nursing facility was top notch, from the rich carpeted floor, to the antique wing chairs and bed, Jolie made sure that her grandfather was kept in a way he'd never been entitled to before. Nearly half her paycheck went to supplement his social security and insurance in order to pay for it, but she couldn't have settled for less.

"Um, I'm sorry I haven't been to visit for a while. You see, a lot's been happening lately." She bit her bottom lip, counting nearly two weeks since her last visit. "A lot going on at the firehouse…then there's Darby. I've been helping her out as much as she'll let me. Which—you know Darby—is precious little, but I do what I can, on the sly, of course. If she knew I had an ulterior motive, she'd send me packing faster than last week's garbage."

She smiled at him, then glanced out the cheval window and the brilliant fall foliage visible just beyond. A blue jay flitted from a nearby branch, squawking. Jolie pretended an interest in it, then slowly looked back toward her grandfather.

"But that's not really why I came all the way out here in the middle of the week, during a workday at that." She bit her lip to stop it from trembling. "You see, there's something I need to talk to somebody about or else I'm afraid I'll burst." She drew in a ragged breath. "You see, Dusty's back."

Jolie gazed at Gramps, her heart contracting so painfully she nearly gasped.

She wasn't sure what she wanted him to say. That is, if he were capable of saying anything at all. But for the first time since he'd had a massive stroke three years ago, she longed for some sort of response. Some sign that he could hear her. That he could understand what she was saying.

She tucked her hair behind her ear and stared into her lap. She and her grandfather had never gotten on well. Vinegar and oil, is what Gramps used to compare them to. Though she'd never been quite clear on who was the vinegar and who the oil, and wasn't sure she wanted to know. Either it meant she was tart and combative. Or slick and evasive. Neither held much appeal to her.

Still, Gramps was her family. The only blood relative she'd known since she was six. The only one she had left now, no matter his condition.

She fought to keep her voice even, knowing it was imperative that she not indicate too much upset in case he could understand and might suffer distress himself.

She clenched her hands tightly in her lap, wondering not for the first time what it must be like to be trapped in a body that no longer worked properly.

She rolled her eyes to stare at the ceiling to stem the tide of tears that seared the back of her eyelids. "I know I told you that Dusty had gone out of town for a while. But I...I didn't tell you the whole truth." She bit soundly on her bottom lip. "He wants a divorce, Gramps. Dusty wants to end our five-year marriage."

She sat like that for long, quiet moments. Staring at the ceiling. Concentrating on breathing in and out. Distantly aware that saying the words hadn't resulted in the stopping of her heart. That she was still very much there. Alive. The trees continued to sway outside the window. The quiet clink of dishes as a cart was rolled by outside the open door reminded her that life went on around her.

She swallowed hard, almost wishing that the world had stopped spinning. It might make the whole mess she was in the middle of much easier to cope with. "I don't know. A part of me thinks I should just give him what he wants. End this…suffering. This pain."

Her quiet gulp filled the silent room.

"Another part…well another part wants to believe that we still have a chance, you know? That maybe, just maybe, if we spend time together, try to talk things out, remember…how good it used to be that…well, that we'll rediscover that common bond that's always existed between us."

Her throat threatened to close up on her, making a strange strangling sound. "But I keep thinking that I can't make Dusty love me if he doesn't."

For long moments she sat, trying to regain control over the tears flowing freely down her cheeks, the breath-stealing ache in her chest. She scrubbed her palms over her damp cheeks, then gave a quiet, humorless laugh. "You know what's funny? I'm sitting here right now, watching you like this…thinking of all Darby has gone through, and I'm feeling…so completely selfish. Guilty that I'm complaining about anything." She took a ragged breath. "After all, I still have my health, don't I? And while I may have lost Dusty, he's not dead. He…he just doesn't want to be married anymore. He just doesn't want me anymore."

She turned her head toward the window, staring sightlessly at the shifting tree branches.

She tried to imagine what Gramps might say. Would he point an accusatory finger at her, pinning her as the one to blame for the end of her marriage? Or would he curse Dusty Conrad? She couldn't be sure. She'd never been very good at second-guessing others' motivations, thoughts. Her own devastating shock at Dusty's departure was a perfect example of that.

Perhaps it was better that Gramps was unable to answer her. She was having a difficult-enough time trying to sort through her own feelings without piling up someone else's on top of them.

Jolie couldn't be sure how long she'd sat there listening to her grandfather's even breathing. Clenching and unclenching her hands in her lap. Trying to make sense out of what was happening in her life and why. But she slowly became aware of a certain resolve stealing over her. An acceptance, really, that what was happening was physically survivable. And if it was physically survivable, well, then, it was up to her to get through the emotional part.

She absently pulled her hair back from her face and sniffed, rubbing the remainder of her tears from her chin. She also realized that while Dusty had been away, she'd never really come to terms with the fact that he might not ever come back to her. With him physically absent, it had been easy to just push the whole issue aside. Pretend that he was on that extended trip out of town to make some extra cash, as she had told everyone, and that he would soon be coming home.

But now that he had come back, and it was crystal clear he had no intention of staying, the time had finally come for her to face the truth. And stare down six months of delayed grieving over the most important relationship of her life.

She glanced back toward her grandfather lying still in the bed. The crisp white linen sheets and his silken blanket had been neatly folded across his chest. His arms lay unmoving at his sides. His eyes stared blindly at the ornate detailing that edged the white ceiling. He hadn't moved a muscle since she'd come in. He hadn't moved a muscle in three years.

She smiled shakily. "God, what a load to dump into your lap all at once, huh?" She slowly got up from the chair, keeping her gaze on his expressionless face. "Sorry about that. It's just that I didn't know who else to talk to. Darby...well, Darby's got enough going on in her life without having to worry about me, too. And Dusty, he...he was always my best friend. My rock. But not anymore." She slid her fingers under her grandfather's and grasped his warm, dry hand in hers. "The only other person I could think of was you." She squeezed his fingers. "God, right now I miss you more than I ever have, Gramps." She choked back a sob. "I could really use some of your no-nonsense advice right about now. No matter how wrong it probably would have been."

She began to slip her hand from beneath his when she grew aware of the slightest pressure, as if he was trying to communicate with her by gripping her. Her heart skipped a beat as she stared at their intertwined fingers. His skin was pale and spotted. Hers chapped and firm. She closed her eyes, trying to discern movement. But after a long moment she had to accept that the motion was either involuntary or she had imagined it.

She placed her other hand over the top of their joined ones, then leaned over to kiss his pasty cheek, pausing a moment to rest her temple against his. "I love you, Gramps," she whispered.

Then she withdrew her hands and slowly stepped from the too silent room, knowing she really hadn't accomplished anything by coming here. But feeling better just the same.

Dusty jerkily looked down at his watch, then tapped the crystal when he discovered it was only three minutes later than the last time he'd checked.

Jolie was more than an hour late.

He rubbed a hand over his face and considered switching on the heat under the soup again, the late lunch turning into dinner. A low meow caught his attention. He looked down to catch Spot forming perfect figure eights around his ankles. "What, the food at the station not good enough for you?" he asked the black-and-white feline.

When he'd opened the door to the house after returning from the hospital, he'd been surprised when Spot zipped inside in front of him. While it was known the fearless feline—who suffered from a severe identity crisis and thought she was a dog—got around town, she'd never actually moved beyond their front porch swing during her visits. That she was not only in the house now, but stuck like glue to the hem of his jeans, caused his concern to double.

Stepping over the cat, Dusty grasped the telephone receiver and pressed the button for the fire station.

The line was picked up on the first ring, and he said, "Martinez? Hey, it's Dusty. Jolie around?"

"Jolie? No…we haven't seen her since the fire. In fact, we were all just wagering on what the two of you were doing right about now."

Dusty absorbed the news. He'd been convinced she'd gotten caught up with something at the station. To find out that she hadn't even gone there, as she said she would, caused his stomach to line with caustic acid.

"Hey, Dus, is she okay? I mean, everything checked out all right at the hospital, didn't it?"

"Yeah. Everything's fine," he said, and hoped like hell it was true. "If she happens by there, have her give me a call at the house, will you?"

Martinez started staying something more, but Dusty firmly placed the phone back in its cradle.

For long moments he stood, weighing where Jolie could have gone, what might have happened. Then he picked up the receiver again and dialed the hospital. He'd put through a request to speak to Tuck when he heard the sound of a familiar car in the drive. Once the hospital operator put him on hold, he hung up the receiver. He turned, waiting as the front door opened then closed. Finally Jolie was standing in the kitchen doorway, her cheeks pink from the autumn chill, her gaze strangely penetrating.

"Hi," he said, thinking the greeting lame, but he was at odds on how else to handle the situation. Surely he more than anyone knew that the last person Jolie had to account for her time to was him. Still, that didn't stop the tension rising in his gut caused by his worry about her.

"Hey," she responded, then shrugged out of his denim jacket and hung it on the back of a chair. He couldn't help noticing the way her fingers caressed the soft, worn cotton, then she seemed to snatch them away from the material, as if caught doing something she shouldn't be doing.

Dusty cleared his throat and forced himself to turn back toward the soup. He switched on the heat under the pan. "I, um, was worried about you."

He wondered if he should tell her he'd just called the station and was in the middle of calling the hospital when she'd returned, then decided against it. Above and beyond everything else, there had always been honesty between them. And he needed to test that honesty now.

He was surprised when she joined him at the counter, taking plates and bowls out from the cupboard and piling the sandwiches he'd made onto one of the plates. "Yeah. I, um, went out to visit Gramps."

Dusty released a breath he hadn't been aware he'd been holding as he recognized her response as the truth. "How is he?"

A shadow crossed behind her eyes as she gathered napkins and opened the silverware drawer. "The same." She hesitated.

Dusty pretended not to notice the way she lingered over the drawer. When he'd returned to the house, he'd put the divorce papers right back where she'd left them, in the drawer. And he didn't doubt it was those papers she now stared at.

He heard the crinkling of paper, then the closing of the drawer. She edged around him, the scent of smoke lingering in her wake. Dusty swallowed hard, watching her out of the corner of his eye as she slowly set the table. "I know it's going to sound funny," she said quietly, "but I could have sworn he understood what I was saying. Sensed that he…heard me."

He nodded, strictly because he didn't know what else to do.

What had she needed to talk to her grandfather about? What was so important that she'd driven an hour-and-a-half round trip to the outskirts of Toledo to speak to a man incapable of responding to her?

Then it hit him. She'd gone out there simply because there was nowhere else for her to go.

He didn't know why, but the realization that he'd lost his role as Jolie's number one confidant cut deep.

Of course she wouldn't turn to him. If for no other reason than he hadn't been around for her to turn to for the past six months.

And was he sure that it was wise to want to regain her trust now? To offer himself up as that guy she used to tell her deepest, darkest secrets to when he knew he'd be leaving again?

If not him, who? a voice asked.

That wasn't his concern. Not anymore. But the reminder refused to take root, much less hold.

He filled the bowls with soup, switched off the burner, then carried the bowls to the table. Jolie followed with the sandwiches.

"Jolie, I…"

She looked at him expectantly, both of them standing behind their chairs. He gripping the ladder back tightly, she with her hands stoically at her sides.

"What is it?" she asked quietly. Too quietly.

He began to open his mouth, even though he didn't know what he planned to say, when the sound of another car engine pulling up into the drive caught their attention.

Dusty tightened his grip on the chair as Jolie broke eye contact, then stared through the open kitchen door toward the front of the house.

A moment later, there was a knock at the front door followed by silence. No cheery call out. No opening of the door to let the visitor in.

That, more than anything, told Dusty the visit was serious.

Jolie briefly met his gaze, then led the way to the foyer. She pushed back the curtain on the side window. Over her shoulder, Dusty made out the side of a county van in the gathering dusk. Children's Services, the lettering read.

Jolie fumbled to quickly open the door, her hands visibly shaking.

Dusty didn't know what he expected to find, but the last thing was Nancy Pollard, whom he remembered as little more than a girl two years behind him in college, standing there holding Eleanor Johansen's hand, staring at them hopefully.

"May we come in?" Nancy asked.

Jolie nodded, then opened the door wider, as though surprised she hadn't already asked them. "Sure, sure. Come on in."

Dusty stepped aside as Nancy led the way inside, toting Ellie along with her. He looked into the little girl's eyes, shuddering when he found the same coal-black look in them.

"I'm sorry to just show up on your doorstep like this, Jolie and Dusty," Nancy said. "But after reviewing my files, and seeing that you both have gone through foster-parent training...well, you're my only option. Would you mind keeping Eleanor until we can work out something else?"

Chapter 9

Jolie felt as though her heart might pound right through her chest as she stared at Nancy Pollard, who hadn't dropped by for a social visit, or on behalf of one cause or another, but rather in her duty as a children's services rep. Jolie's gaze swept to Dusty, then to the girl standing in her foyer as if in a trance, her face expressionless, her hand held loosely by Nancy.

"Excuse me?" Jolie whispered, certain she hadn't heard correctly.

Dusty stepped forward. "Why don't you let me take your coats," he said, smiling especially warmly at Ellie as he waited out her reluctance, then helped her off with a purple-and-white parka. Jolie only absently registered that Nancy had come up with some secondhand clothes for Ellie to wear. Nowhere to be seen was the soot-covered nightgown she'd had on earlier, the only personal item she'd taken from the fire, and only then because she'd been wearing it.

Dusty then accepted Nancy's black vinyl raincoat and hung it along with Ellie's in the hall closet. "Jolie and I were just sitting down to a light dinner. Ellie, would you like to nibble on something?" He held his hand out to her. She took it, but not with enthusiasm. Instead there seemed to be a fatalistic automation to her movements as she followed Dusty toward the kitchen.

Jolie looked at Nancy, then followed. In the doorway of the kitchen she watched Dusty settle Ellie into a chair, then place a small bowl of soup and half a sandwich in front of her, although the girl looked about as interested in the food as the color of the walls. He switched on the television on the counter, turning the channels until he found a cartoon of some sort or another.

Then he crouched down in front of Ellie. "We're just going to be in the other room, okay, Ellie? Not ten feet away. Come get us if you need anything, all right?"

The little girl nodded solemnly, her eyes fastened on the cartoon, though Jolie wondered if she really saw it.

As soon as the three of them stood back in the living room, Nancy cleared her throat. "Thanks. This isn't something Eleanor needed to hear and normally not something I would handle in front of her. It's just…well, this case has me so rattled, you know. I lived on the same block as Jeff Johansen growing up and…well, my objectivity is a little on the shy side right now."

Jolie nodded, her heart going out to her. She'd felt the same way during the fire. "That's all right."

With Ellie out of the way, Dusty's stance completely changed. Far from looking like a man in control, he appeared ill at ease somehow. "I'm sorry, Nancy, but I don't think we can help you."

Jolie's stomach pitched to her feet. She opened her mouth to speak, but no sound came out.

"Please just hear me out." Nancy cleared her throat, then rifled through her barely creased briefcase, producing a sheaf of papers. "With Jeff Johansen in the hospital, we need someone to look after Eleanor. As I'm sure you are both aware, neither Jeff nor Angela have any living relatives. At least not any in a position to take care of a five-year-old. Which puts us in a bit of a bind." Nancy smiled. "I want you to look after her."

Jolie's heart thudded loudly in her ears. "Of course."

"I don't think that's a good idea," Dusty said at the same time.

Nancy blinked, looking between them both, her smile vanishing. "Normally I wouldn't even think to ask you to do this. While my files show that you both completed foster-parenting courses eight months ago, they also show that you've never fostered." She held up the papers, then awkwardly moved to tuck them back into her case. "For the record, do you mind telling me why not?"

"I've been out of town," Dusty said.

"I see." Nancy craned her head toward the kitchen. Jolie couldn't make out anything and suspected Nancy couldn't, either. "Look, I'd never dream of asking you to do this unless I didn't have any other choice. It'll be only one…two nights tops, until I can figure out where to place Eleanor more permanently."

Jolie made a small sound. "More permanently?"

She nodded and briefly bit on her bottom lip. "I've consulted with the physicians in charge at the hospital. Things are, well, pretty touch-and-go with Jeff right now. And even if…" Her voice cracked and she cleared her throat again. "When Jeff does pull through, he's facing an extended hospital stay and extensive rehabilitation therapy. He can't possibly look after Eleanor himself."

Jolie caught Dusty about to say something and quickly reached out to touch his arm. "Nancy, would you excuse us a moment?"

The children's services rep looked suddenly rattled. "Um, sure. Of course." She gestured uncertainly, then moved in the direction of the kitchen. "Why don't I go sit with Eleanor. You know, so you can have some privacy."

Jolie smiled softly at her. "Thank you. We shouldn't be more than a few minutes."

As soon as Nancy's footsteps disappeared down the hall and Jolie heard her speaking softly to Ellie, she wrapped her arms around her midsection and closed her eyes.

"Jolie, I…"

She held up a trembling hand. "Please, don't say anything. Not this moment. I need to think."

She couldn't bear to open her eyes. View the question in Dusty's eyes. She knew he wanted to turn Nancy and little Ellie away. She also knew why.

The young woman apparently didn't know of their…separation. Then again, why would she? As far as the town knew, Dusty had resigned from the fire station to take a more lucrative construction position in Toledo. Nothing more, nothing less. If they had questions as to why this was the first time he'd been home in six months, they didn't pose them to her. If they found it curious that she'd never gone to visit him, they never breathed a word.

Amazing how easily one accepted a lie because the truth was too difficult to swallow. Everyone, herself included, found it preferable to think that what had happened between her and Dusty was temporary. That now that he was back, everything would go back to being right again.

"I need to take her, Dusty," she whispered, finally opening her eyes and looking at him.

She almost wished she hadn't. "I don't think it's a good idea, Jol."

"Why?" she asked, tightening her arms.

He glanced away. "You know why."

"Because you're leaving?"

He shifted his weight from his right to his left foot, then shoved his hands into his front jeans pockets. "That…and more."

"Because you're afraid that my inability to bear you kids might be behind my need to do this?"

His gaze snapped to hers and she knew instantly it was true.

"Look, Dusty, neither of those issues factor into my desire to look after Ellie." She paced a short way away, her back to him. "I know you're leaving. You don't have to tell me that. I also know that I'm infertile. Your reminding me of that doesn't change that, either."

"But you need my consent."

She looked at him over her shoulder.

"Okay, maybe *consent* is the wrong word. Perhaps silence is more the description I'm looking for." He sighed and rubbed his hand over his face. "Both you and I know Nancy wouldn't even be here if…"

Jolie swallowed. "If she knew the truth about us?"

He averted her gaze. "Yes."

Jolie knew it was true. While it wasn't unheard-of for single parents to take in a foster child, assigning a single woman to look after a five-year-old was probably far from the norm.

She turned her head back toward the darkened front window. "Look, Dusty, I can't pretend to understand what you're thinking right now. Maybe you believe this might be some sort of ploy on my behalf to try to get you to stay." She winced at the words. "But it's not. What I can tell you is that I know what I'm feeling. And right now that's the need to look after that little girl in there. To help her past the shock she's feeling after losing her mother…her house…knowing her father might not make it." Her voice dropped to a whisper. "And I know I can do that. If…" Her voice cracked. "If for no other reason than because I've been there."

She turned pleading eyes on him, but he still wasn't looking at her. She stepped eagerly forward and grasped his arms in her hands. "I know what she's feeling right now, Dusty. I know what it's like to have your whole world fall apart around your ears. To think that God must have some sort of personal vendetta against you…if you're not already questioning whether there is a God or not. I see. I understand. I can help."

He looked at her, his eyes full of inexplicable emotion. "Or you'll die trying."

She slowly released her grip.

He restlessly ran his hand over his hair. "Jolie, I don't object to this because I think you're incapable of doing exactly what you're saying. I was there, too. Remember?"

How could she forget? Dusty's face was the first friendly one she saw when she was carried from the house over the shoulder of a fireman.

"I just don't think…this is a great idea right now."

She smiled sadly. "You're going to have to do better than that if you hope to talk me out of this."

He grimaced. "Okay. Let's begin with you were one of the firefighters involved in fighting the fire. That you were the one who went into that house and rescued Ellie. That even now you might be blaming yourself for the loss of her mother…the injuries suffered by her father."

Her spine snapped upright, despite the growing acidic feeling in her stomach.

"Then there is the fact that…our marriage is over."

She visibly winced. It was the first time either of them had said it aloud in a concrete way. *Our marriage is over.* No maybes. No perhaps. Merely an inarguable "is."

She battled back the pain spreading throughout her chest cavity like a ragged crack across ice. "Please, Dusty," she whispered, searching his eyes. "I've never asked you to put aside your feelings, to do something for me based simply on trust alone." She realized the truth in her statement even as she said the words. "Never."

A shadow of sadness entered his brown eyes. "Did you ever think that that may have been part of the problem?"

She shivered and tried again. "I'm asking you now, Dusty. Give me these two days. You don't have to stay. I'll sign the...papers. You can leave. I'll just tell them you were called back to work or something."

He shook his head. "No, Jolie. From what I've seen so far, you haven't told anyone about the truth of our situation now. If I agree to this...you may never tell anyone the truth."

She mentally stumbled over that possibility. "I will," she whispered, though even she wasn't convinced by the watery sound of her voice.

Jolie's shoulders sank and she slowly turned away from him. So this was it, then, huh? It took a little girl in need of a temporary home to finally shine a spotlight on the reality of her situation. Her marriage was over.

She felt the heat of his hand before she actually felt his fingers resting first against her shoulder, then the side of her neck.

She resisted the urge to lean into his touch. Just like she had too many times before. "Please, Dusty. This is something I need to do."

His hand stilled and he didn't say anything, for what seemed like forever. "Okay," he said quietly, his fingertips making her sensitive skin tingle. "But if we're going to do this, then I'm going to have to stay here for the duration. We can...we can work the rest of it out in a couple days. When Nancy finds her a more permanent home."

Jolie turned in his arms so quickly she nearly toppled

them both over. She hugged him, her eyes filling with scalding tears as she rested her head against his shoulder.

At first, it appeared as if he didn't know what to do. His arms lay limply against her hips. Then he curved his hands around her back, pressing his fingers firmly against her spine. She could have sworn she heard a low groan deep in his chest.

"Thank you," she whispered. "Thank you for this, Dusty."

Chapter 10

Dusty quietly climbed the steps to the second floor. Dusk had long since settled and he used the light from the foyer to guide his way. After a long, trying evening with Ellie, they'd put the shell-shocked five-year-old to bed in the guest bedroom a little more than an hour ago. He came to a stop at the top of the stairs. And this was the fourth time in that same hour that Jolie had stolen away to gaze upon the girl from the open doorway.

Dusty watched as she wrapped her arms around herself and absently squeezed. His throat contracted around a swallow, and the shallow sound brought her head around to face him.

He managed a smile. "Any change?"

She quietly pulled the door until only a few inches

remained between the edge and the jamb, then met him at the top of the stairs. "She finally appears to have fallen off to sleep. I…I wanted to wipe the tears from her cheeks, but I was afraid I'd wake her up again."

He nodded.

Earlier, while they were all downstairs, he and Jolie had tried to make everything appear as normal as possible, attempting to gently draw Ellie out from her state of shock. But Ellie had been minimally responsive; the little girl had kept a deceptively calm mask in place. She'd even obediently eaten a light dinner of spaghetti. But after they had shown her upstairs to the guestroom, where there wasn't one stuffed animal, not one item that was familiar to her, Ellie had silently begun to cry the instant she thought they had left the room.

"Nancy says she's contacting a child psychologist first thing in the morning," Jolie said quietly, as if reading his mind.

"Fat amount of good that's going to do us now." He rubbed the back of his neck. "But at least she's finally sleeping."

She nodded. "Yes."

He motioned for her to precede him down the stairs, and she led the way back to the kitchen, where she fixed herself a cup of hot cocoa then asked if he wanted anything. He shook his head and took a beer from the refrigerator. She leaned against the island, slowly sipping from her cup. He popped the cap off the beer and took a long swallow, staring off into space. The only sound was the tick-tick of the old grandfather clock in the foyer. And the overly loud purr of Spot, where she was curled up on one of the chair cushions, fast asleep. The cat had seemed to take up residence in their home. Strange, since she'd never shown much interest in the place before.

Jolie shifted, the rustle of her clothes loud in the quiet room. "Do you think what we're feeling right now is natural?" she asked.

He looked up to find her staring through the back window. "What would that be?"

She absently shrugged as if unsure, herself, how she felt. "I don't know. So...helpless. Powerless to take away little Ellie's ghosts and fill her mind and heart with all things light and happy."

She glanced at him and he smiled. "I'd say it's natural. And not just for us. I imagine all parents feel that way when something traumatic happens to one of their children."

She glanced quickly away at his mention of the word *parents*. He squinted at her, watching as she ran the tip of her index finger along the rim of her mug.

"What is it?" he asked.

She quietly cleared her throat. "Do you, you know, think it would have made a difference if we had been able to have children of our own?"

There it was. The exact question he'd been dreading. The number one reason why he hadn't thought it a good idea for Jolie to take in Ellie. Not with all that was going on between the two of them now. Not given the unstable emotional state she was in as a result.

She sighed and rolled her eyes toward the ceiling. "I'm not asking for the reason you think, Dusty. And I'm certainly not looking to place any blame, or make excuses. I'm just…curious."

"Hmm…curious."

She nodded, her eyes wide over the mug as she took a small sip.

He leaned a little more comfortably against the counter, then crossed his boots at the ankles. "I really don't know, Jolie. I suppose things would be…different if we had kids."

She nodded, as if expecting his answer.

He grimaced and took another long swallow of beer, agitatedly rolling the bottle between his palms. "That doesn't mean I wouldn't have left."

She looked at him, surprise lighting the blue depths of her eyes.

He cursed under his breath. "Let me ask you a question, Jolie. How do you think being a mother would have changed you?"

She slowly placed her mug down, saying nothing for long moments. "How do you mean?"

"Would you have quit the force? Opted to be a stay-at-home mom? Cut back your hours?" *Do as I asked you and leave firefighting behind altogether?*

"I don't know," she said quietly.

He finished off the beer in record time, then tossed the bottle into the garbage can under the sink. "Let's face it. We can stand here all night rehashing what life would have been like if only this had happened. If only we'd done that. But the fact is that we can't change things. Not now. What's done is done and there's no altering that."

He began to pass her on his way out to the living room and the television, where he hoped something would be capable of taking his mind off their current conversation.

She grasped his arm, halting his progress. "What are you talking about, Dusty? Us? Are you saying that there's no changing the course for us?" He gazed into her questioning eyes, feeling more drawn to her now that they'd made love than he had before. Maybe because he'd been reminded of how wonderful it felt to have her legs wrapped around his waist. To feel her mouth responding under his. To know that on some level they would always be a couple. "Or are you talking about Erick?"

She couldn't have shocked him more had she just landed a sucker punch to his solar plexus.

"What?"

She stared at where her hand still rested against his arm, then slowly pulled it away. "You know, we never really did talk much about Erick after...well, after he died." She smiled, but there was a sad slant to it. "I guess we were too caught up in our own problems."

He stiffened. "No. It's because there's nothing there to talk about."

Her feathery brows pulled together in a frown. "Isn't there?" She tucked her hair behind her ear, her gaze dropping to the floor. "You know, I can't tell you how many nights I've lain awake, wondering about what happened to us. Trying to fit the pieces together." She sucked in her lips, then released them. "But there was always this missing piece, you know? Some elusive reason behind your actions that I just couldn't seem to put my finger on." Her gaze swept back to his. "I never even thought it might be Erick."

Dusty's muscles bunched, a self-protective anger beginning to stir in his stomach. "I don't know what you're talking about, Jolie."

He issued an order to his feet to move, to get out of that kitchen as fast as his legs would carry him. But his muscles ignored him.

"Don't you?" she asked softly. "It wasn't too long ago that I would have said the same thing. That there was no way that one thing was connected to the other. But it took Darby dropping by yesterday afternoon, and seeing how you reacted to her, to make it hit home. To finally move the clouds from in front of my eyes so I could see that Erick's death has a lot more to do with what's happening between us than either of us believed."

Dusty clenched his jaw. "You're reaching."

She shook her head, her gaze steady. "I don't think I am."

He opened his mouth to respond and she held her hand up to stop him. "No. Please don't lash out and try to make this seem like some desperate attempt on my part to get you to stay, Dusty. I couldn't handle that. Not right now. Not with everything else going on." She bit briefly on the flesh of her bottom lip. "The fact is, I've accepted that our marriage is over. All that remains is crossing the t's and dotting the i's. You want out, I'm letting you out."

His heart contracted so tightly it was suddenly impossible to breathe.

"I'm just trying to finally put all this together. To understand the whys. Until I do that…we both do that…then there's really no closure, is there? Even long after you've gone, there will always be that mysterious something hanging over both our heads. That question looming between us, no matter where we are physically."

"Maybe you'll have questions. I have none."

She openly flinched, her pain at his remark evident. "If that's so true then why…why did you kiss me yesterday morning? Why did you…make love to me?"

Her point hit home as accurately as a poison-tipped arrow.

She made a small sound in her throat. "Let me guess. You're putting it down as hormones run amok. As your having gone without sex for so long that it was only natural that you were drawn to me. Or how about this. You wanted one last time to remember me by. Or, worse yet, you wanted to give *me* something to remember."

Dusty had his jawed clenched together so tightly he couldn't have spoken if he wanted to.

She tilted her head slightly, her gaze solidly fastened on his face. "You know what I'm beginning to think? It's none of the above. What happened yesterday neither one of us expected. And while, yes, it's probably easier, maybe even wiser, to pretend it never happened, the fact is that it did. And I think we owe it to each other, to ourselves, to find the reason before we say goodbye to…us forever."

Dusty rubbed his jaw. "And if the reason is just momentary lust?"

She lifted her chin in that stubborn way that made

him want to kiss her all over again. "Then at least we'll know the truth."

He nodded. "Okay. Maybe you're right. Maybe we do have to take a closer look at things."

She cleared her throat. "Including Erick?"

An image of his brother's stiff, unmoving body lying at the funeral home flashed across his mind, followed quickly by the image of Jolie lying in that hospital bed, as still and as white as snow. "No."

He stalked from the room, but rather than going into the living room as he initially planned, he headed instead for the front door. The instant he was standing on the porch, he dragged in huge lungfuls of the crisp, cool night air, but nothing could clear the turmoil from his mind and heart.

Dusty carefully positioned the last square of cobalt-blue porcelain tile on the base of the Jacuzzi, shifting it into place, then wiping the mortar away. When he'd returned to the house, he found Jolie asleep on the couch, the television flickering in front of her. Her upright position told him she'd probably been waiting for him. Likely to discuss those things she'd outlined in the kitchen earlier. But rather than waking her, he pulled the stadium blanket from the back of the recliner and covered her with it, then disappeared upstairs to the master bathroom, doing those things that wouldn't disturb Jolie or Ellie.

Now, three hours later, he'd finished tiling the base of the tub, and spots were dancing in front of his eyes from two nights of very little sleep and a whole load of questions.

He pushed back onto his heels then stood, stepping to wash his hands in the new sink. He caught sight of himself in the white-edged oval mirror and ran his damp fingers over his hair. He looked like hell. Worse, he felt like hell. And the damnable thing about it was that he didn't see any clear-cut way out of it.

He recognized that one of the reasons he'd been so upset earlier was because Jolie was right. There was too much unfinished business, too many unanswered questions looming between them, for them to just turn their backs on each other, on their marriage, and continue on to another life.

Of course, Jolie usually was right. Which further agitated him. Not because he begrudged her her insight. No. Rather it made him see how much he'd been hiding from her. Hiding from even himself.

He turned back to the work area, scraping the excess cement mortar from the old plastic bowl with the trowel and tossing it into the garbage, then cleaning up, the process of rubbing the adhesive from the newly positioned tile somewhat calming.

Jolie was also right in that they'd never really discussed Erick's death beyond the obvious. He could say it was because of all that was going on at the time. Jolie's own injuries. His decision to quit the department. But now that Jolie had shone the spotlight directly on him, it wasn't so easy to lie to himself. Truthfully, he hadn't been able to talk about Erick then. To discuss what he'd felt. To explore what impact losing his brother had had on his life.

And he wasn't at all certain if he could do so now.

When he'd left the house earlier, he'd done so with no set destination. He'd climbed into his truck and just driven. But when he'd found himself on the road leading out to his brother's...to Darby's ranch outside of town, he'd decided that maybe his sister-in-law could give him the insight he was looking for. He'd pulled up the long, winding gravel drive and found Darby sitting on the front porch, a blanket wrapped around her shoulders to ward off the cold, the twins asleep inside the house.

For an hour they'd talked about everything but what was happening between him and Jolie. The twins' school woes. The myriad animals that inhabited the ranch and kept being added to. Dusty had just been about to ask Darby about Erick, about how his dying had affected her, when the sheriff's car pulled up behind his truck. John Sparks had been on his way home, spotted Dusty and decided to stop and say hello.

The hello had lasted another hour before Dusty decided to head back into town.

Now, as he finished his clean-up, he tossed the cloth he'd used aside, then rose to his feet and stepped to the door. There was nothing more he could do without using a power drill, a hammer or a saw. And considering that they'd had such a difficult time getting Ellie to drop off to sleep, he decided to call it quits for the night.

He switched off the light in the bath, then crossed the dark bedroom floor, his footsteps muffled by the carpeting, refusing to look at the bed he and Jolie had once shared to see if she'd made it up. Instead, he went downstairs. And found her in exactly the same spot he had when he'd returned from Darby's.

For long moments he stood there admiring her. Taking in the soft way her light brown hair lay against her cheek. The proud jut of her chin, even in sleep. The quiet sound of her breathing.

"Oh, Jolie, what happened to us," he murmured.

He moved closer to her, to straighten the blanket that had shifted and now lay around her waist. As he did, he noticed that something had changed since he'd first spotted her sitting there asleep. He frowned and moved even closer, noticing the fresh tracks of tears down her creamy skin, her damp, spiky lashes revealing that Ellie wasn't the only one haunted by demons he could never hope to understand.

Jolie had always been one to put herself on the line, physically, in her career as a firefighter, and emotionally, as she did now by taking in a damaged little girl who would inevitably bring raw memories of her own rushing back. It's what he loved about her. It's what he hated about her. And it's what ceaselessly drew him to her like a fascinated fly into her mysterious, silken web. He wanted to understand her. To study her. To be like her. He remembered once thinking that Jolie Calbert personified the definition of a true hero.

How could a person be so selfless? Be willing to risk so much and at the same time sacrifice everything for others? He'd looked for the same qualities in himself and had come up empty. Yes, he'd fought fires. But he'd done so more for the adrenaline rush, the sheer thrill of fighting the monster, than for the need to help others. Oh, saving someone was unlike any other emotion, but it hadn't been what had driven him.

Then there was Jolie, whose every deed seemed dictated by some impossible, fathomless desire to help others. Even at the expense of herself. Even at the expense of their marriage.

Before he could question the action, he quietly lifted the blanket and slid to sit on the sofa, then gently shifted her so that she lay against his side. Automatically, she curled in closer, making a soft humming sound in her sleep.

Dusty's chest filled with a pervasive warmth as he curved a hand down her back and pulled her even closer. They'd always seemed to fit so well together. He remembered thinking that the first time he'd held her. It had been their third date and they'd spent the evening at the county fair, sharing barbecue ribs, standing in line for the rides, rocking the Ferris wheel car until Jolie finally begged for mercy. Then he'd taken her home to her grandfather's house. It was there on the front step that he'd been unable to stop himself from kissing her. And, oh, how good she had tasted. Like pink cotton candy, saltwater taffy and one-hundred-percent woman. And just like now, she had curved against him. Her breasts pressing against his chest. Her chin against his collarbone. In that one moment he'd felt as if he'd found home for the first time.

Jolie moved, tucking her head beneath his chin so that her sweet hair teased his nose with its freshly washed scent. It was at times like these that he could almost forget about the problems that existed between them. Convince himself that there were so many things right, there couldn't possibly be enough wrong to warrant his leaving.

Almost.

He closed his eyes and took a deep breath. But he didn't want to think about that. Not right now. He merely wanted to feel the heat of Jolie's body against his, listen to the soft sounds of her sleeping, and remember what it was like to just be.

Chapter 11

Jolie slowly became aware of the sound of a distant meow. She wrinkled her nose and burrowed into the covers, feeling toasty and warm and safe. But she and Dusty didn't have a cat, she thought. Must be the neighbor's, she rationalized.

A dull pain shot up her neck and she winced. Now, why… Then she realized that she wasn't in a prone position, lying in the comfort of her bed. And of course she and Dusty didn't have a cat. She didn't even have Dusty anymore.

She frowned. Then why did she feel him against her side, warm and hard?

The sound of meowing became louder. Jolie popped open her eyes, becoming aware of two more things simultaneously. That she and Dusty must have slept together on the couch overnight. And that Ellie had awakened before either of them and was standing there watching them, Spot clutched tightly in her arms.

"What? What is it?" Dusty asked, abruptly awakening, as well.

Jolie braced her hand against his chest and pushed herself up to a sitting position. "I think it's morning." She swallowed and smiled at the long-faced little girl. "Hi, Ellie. Have you been waiting long?"

At first there was no response. Then she slowly shook her head.

"I'm glad." Jolie made sure her shirt and jeans were fastened, then tried to fix her hair. "My, we must have fallen asleep watching television."

Dusty stretched next to her and chuckled. She resisted the urge to elbow him in the ribs.

"Have you ever done that, Ellie? Fallen asleep while watching a show or a movie?"

This time she nodded.

Which was a good sign. Wasn't it? Jolie couldn't seem to think straight, her head was crowded with sleep, her eyes blinded by the bright morning sunlight shining through the window. Of course, Ellie hadn't actually spoken since Nancy dropped her off yesterday. In fact, she hadn't said a single, solitary word since Jolie had found her hiding behind the pillows on her bed yesterday. But that was normal, wasn't it?

Spot meowed again and Jolie blinked, bringing the black-and-white scrap of fur into focus. She instantly discovered the cause for the noise. Ellie wasn't so much as holding the cat as she was crushing her.

Jolie began to reach out, then took her hand back.

Next to her, Dusty sat up. "Good morning, Ellie." He grinned at her in a way that warmed Jolie's heart. "Good morning, Spot." He reached out. "May I?" he asked Ellie, indicating he wanted to take the cat. "I'd like to give Spot a little morning cuddle, as well."

The girl began to back away, then seemed to change her mind and awkwardly started to hold the feline out. Dusty swooped the cat up. "Hey, there, Spotster. Did you sleep well?" He scratched the cat under her chin and instantly the meows turned to purring. Jolie watched Ellie watching Dusty. "Are you hungry? I know I sure am."

Jolie glanced at her watch. It was just a little past seven and she knew an instant of panic. Until she realized today was her regular day off. "Hmm, what sounds better to you? Eggs and bacon? Or pancakes and sausage?"

Ellie didn't say anything. She glanced at Dusty, who was putting down Spot out of Ellie's reach. Immediately the cat scampered on toward the kitchen, as if aware of the conversation and determined to be first in line for some grub.

Jolie hummed. "Then again, I think we have some good old cornflakes in the cupboard."

"Pancakes," Ellie said quietly.

Jolie smiled at her. "Well, then. I guess pancakes it is, then."

There was a brief knock at the door, then the sound of the knob being jimmied. Jolie raised her brows, keeping eye contact with the girl. "Well, who do you suppose that is so early? And do you think they want some pancakes, too?"

She couldn't be sure, but she thought she saw Ellie's deep blue eyes light up. If only briefly.

Jolie pushed from the couch and started for the door even as Dusty led Ellie toward the kitchen. She looked through the side window, immediately spotting Mrs. Noonan from across the street.

Jolie briefly closed her eyes. No. She really couldn't deal with the busybody right now.

Pushing aside the desire to pretend she was still asleep and not answer the door, she instead opened it and caught Mrs. Noonan leaning over in an effort to peep through the window.

"Good morning, Mrs. Noonan."

"Oh, Lordy, you startled me, Jolie."

She noticed that the older woman held something in her hands and openly considered it.

"I wasn't sure if you were up yet. You know, seeing as you had such a late night and all."

"I'm up," Jolie reassured her, deciding not to comment on or think about how exactly the older woman knew how late they'd been up and wonder if Mrs. Noonan slept for fear of missing something in the neighborhood.

Mrs. Noonan looked as if she was waiting to be invited in, but Jolie purposefully kept the door open to only show herself. "Is there something you wanted, Mrs. Noonan?"

"Wanted? Oh, yes." She held up the foil-covered dish in her hands, then leaned forward and whispered, "I heard about little Eleanor Johansen being dropped off here yesterday. Awfully nice of you and Dusty to agree to look after her. Awfully nice." She thrust the plate toward her. "I just thought that with so much on your hands, that maybe I'd bring something over to help you, you know, foodwise."

"That's kind of you, Mrs. Noonan," Jolie murmured. And it *was* kind of her. She felt more than a tad guilty as she peeked under the foil to see a heaping pile of homemade doughnuts.

"I put colored sprinkles on a few. You know, for the little one."

Jolie smiled. "I'm sure she'll like that."

Mrs. Noonan stood quietly, putting Jolie decisively on the spot.

Jolie cleared her throat. "Um…we were just getting ready to make some pancakes, Mrs. Noonan. Would you like to join us?"

No matter how neighborly the invitation, Jolie found herself cringing. She opened the door in anticipation of Mrs. Noonan saying something along the lines of "Don't mind if I do," then tramping inside.

Instead, she smiled and shook her head. "That's kind of you, Jolie, but I've already eaten." She gestured toward the doughnuts. "You all have a nice breakfast. Oh, and let me know if you need anything, ya hear?"

Her brows high on her forehead, Jolie stared after the older woman as she made her way back across the street, then disappeared into her house.

Shaking her head, she closed the door and went into the kitchen to show the gift to Dusty and Ellie. She removed the foil and placed the antique china plate on the kitchen table, indicating that Ellie should choose whichever one she'd like. She immediately picked the one with the most colored sprinkles.

Jolie smiled as Dusty placed a glass of milk in front of the little girl. "I've already started the pancakes. Why don't you go ahead and catch a shower. I'll take one after."

Jolie glanced around him, finding that he had indeed taken the mix out and was in the middle of measuring the ingredients. "Okay," she said slowly.

Throughout her shower, and breakfast, and the better part of the morning, which included a visit from the child psychologist Nancy had promised, Jolie felt oddly out of sorts. It was the first time in what seemed like forever that she had something else to focus on aside from her own problems. But no matter how hard she tried, or how charming Dusty was, neither of them could seem to draw more from Ellie than a nod or a shake. And the way Spot continued to hang out at the house was…unnerving, to say the least. If she didn't know better, she'd think the canny feline thought she was needed and was determined to hang around until she felt differently.

The rest of the morning wasn't looking like it was going to be much better. Especially after Jolie got the news that Ellie's father was still in ICU, his condition critical. Not even Tucker would level with her and tell her if he personally thought Jeff would pull through.

She and Dusty had decided that the best course of action to take in regard to Ellie with the news of her father was to avoid the subject until they learned something more substantial. Nancy agreed. Getting the child's hopes up, then having her father's health take a turn for the worse, would only further confuse her.

Then there was the entire issue of the death of her mother.

Jolie stood in the doorway of the guest bedroom, eyeing her attempt at making the room look more homey. Dusty had merely shaken his head when she'd returned from a grocery store run with stuffed animals and a cartoon-print bedspread and sheets to make the room more fit for a five-year-old. He didn't have to say anything about the temporary condition of her stay. She already knew that. Instead, she reasoned that since all the Johansen belongings had been destroyed in the fire, Ellie would need the things, anyway.

She rested her temple against the doorjamb, listening to the sounds of cartoons on the living room television, where she knew Ellie was sitting watching impassively. The child psychologist hadn't been able to get Ellie to communicate much, but she had been able to determine that she was aware of the death of her mother and knew her father was in the hospital. Before leaving with a promise to come back in two days, she'd advised Jolie and Dusty not to broach the subject themselves, but that if Ellie indicated a desire to talk about the loss of her mother, or asked about her father's condition, that they should try to be as honest and forthcoming as possible.

But Ellie hadn't communicated with them at all yet and Jolie was beginning to fear she wouldn't, either.

She turned from the doorway and made her way quietly back downstairs, hesitating in front of the living room arch. God, she looked so small. Smaller than even her five years. So much had been heaped on this young girl's shoulders.

Jolie shivered and wrapped her arms around herself, not remembering many details about the time after her parents had died. Except, of course, beyond Dusty's attentiveness, and her grandfather's gruffness. She recalled feeling...numb. As if she'd known how much her life had changed and would continue to change and that things would never be the same again.

She saw those same fatalistic feelings on Ellie's face now.

Spot rubbed against her ankle. She looked down and frowned, increasingly convinced the cat was trying to tell her something, perform some sort of role. She lightly shook her head, telling herself she was losing it as she picked the feline up and petted her. Her instant purring told her all the cat had wanted was attention.

And that perhaps that's what Ellie needed now, too.

Giving Spot a hearty final pat, she put her back down, then entered the living room and sat on the floor next to Ellie, cross-legged.

"Oh, *Scooby-Doo,*" she said. "I used to watch this when I was a kid."

It was a Halloween episode. And the crazy thing about it was that Jolie was convinced she knew the end if she just racked her brain enough for it.

Instead, she waited for the next commercial, then stretched out her legs in front of her. "You know, Halloween's tomorrow night."

Ellie blinked but didn't look at her.

"Did you plan on going trick-or-treating, Ellie?"

No response.

Jolie bit hard on her bottom lip, trying to think of

what her friend Angela, Ellie's mom, would say at a time like this.

"I've got a thought," Jolie said, finally shifting her attention back to the television. "Old Man Peterson has a whole patch full of pumpkins. Wouldn't it be great to go out there and pick one, then come back here and decorate it for Halloween?"

Out of the corner of her eye, she watched for Ellie's response. Nothing but a couple of blinks.

She sighed as if the proposal bored her, as well. "Yeah, it's a pretty lame idea, isn't it?"

The cartoon came back on and Jolie's shoulders slumped in defeat.

She hadn't exactly expected this to be a walk in the park, but she hadn't anticipated it would be so difficult, either. Ellie appeared to have holed herself up in a tiny corner within herself, and it was going to take more than doughnuts, and pancakes, and the promise of carving pumpkins to bring her out.

"I'd like to get a pumpkin," Ellie said.

Jolie blinked at her, wondering if the girl had said the words, or whether she had imagined them. When Ellie kept her head straight, staring at the screen, she was beginning to suspect the latter. Then Ellie turned her wide, bright blue eyes on her, as if expecting an answer.

"Oh!" Jolie said, surprising herself. "Well, then. Why don't you go upstairs to the master bath and tell Dusty where we're going and ask if he'd like to come along while I get our coats?"

Ellie continued staring at her, absolutely no shift in her expression. Jolie smiled patiently, thinking the girl's taking her up on her suggestion would be too much to hope for.

So Jolie went up herself and asked Dusty to come along. He was up to his elbows in Spackle and told her to go on without him. And she did. She and Ellie and Spot—who wasn't pleased that Jolie had planned to leave her behind—drove out to the farm to pick out a pumpkin, Jolie being careful to mark a wide path around Ellie's old neighborhood lest she get a glimpse of the charred remains of the house that had nearly claimed her life. She turned the radio on low to an oldies station, making attempts at conversation, but being careful not to talk too much or try too hard, while Ellie kept her head turned toward the window, gazing out on the bright autumn afternoon and absently patting Spot.

"What?" Jolie wanted to ask the cat when she caught the feline staring at her with a kind of "well, go on, already" expression on her furry face. Which was ridiculous, of course. The cat couldn't possibly have any idea what had happened and what needed to be done to coax Ellie out of her shell.

Before long, the sweeping field came into view, the blobs of orange pumpkins dotting the green, broad-leafed vines, reminding Jolie of Charlie Brown's Great Pumpkin Patch. Ellie didn't seem to notice they'd arrived. Not even after Jolie had pulled the Jeep to a stop near the gate to the field, where a young family was carefully rolling out a monster pumpkin through the opening, their smiles wide, their cheeks pink.

Jolie tightened her grip on the steering wheel. Of course. Why hadn't she thought that this type of outing was something a young family would do together? What had she been thinking? Seeing the other family couldn't help but trigger memories in Ellie of her own broken family.

Stupid, stupid, stupid.

"Look, Jolie…I want that one."

The words were so unexpected, Jolie was startled by them. Her heart beat an erratic rhythm in her chest as she looked hopefully at Ellie, finding the little girl's round face awash with excitement.

She cleared the emotion from her throat and tried to follow her chubby finger. "Which one?"

Her eyes widened as her gaze settled on what had to be the most gigantic pumpkin she'd ever seen. There seemed to be enough room in the sucker for her, Ellie, Dusty and even the irritating cat.

"Hmm," she said carefully. "Somehow I don't think it will fit into the back of the Jeep."

Ellie's eyes immediately dulled and she dropped her hand back to lay limply by her side.

Jolie felt as if the sun had ducked behind a cloud, threatening never to return again.

She smiled. "But hey, we can give it the old college try, can't we?"

Ellie instantly perked up again, reaching for the door handle and sliding out. Spot seemed to give Jolie a long suffering look before leaping out after her.

"What?" she asked the cat. "Would you rather I told her there wasn't a chance in Hades that we're taking that thing home?"

Great, she thought, now she was talking to a cat.

She drew in a deep breath and said a silent prayer.

Please, Old Man Peterson, say you're holding on to the pumpkin for some other reason. Anything but that we can take that mammoth thing home.

She slowly got out of the Jeep, following Ellie's path toward the pumpkin on steroids. As incredible as it seemed, it only got bigger the closer she got to it.

She stuffed her hands into her pockets, trying desperately to find a way out of the mess she'd gotten herself into. "Well," she said. "I bet there's probably enough seeds in there to turn all of Ohio into a pumpkin patch."

Ellie giggled, running her tiny hand over the side of the rippling skin of the orange monstrosity.

Jolie estimated that it had to be at least four feet high and five feet wide, and likely weighed as much as her Jeep.

"We could make lots and lots of pumpkin pies," Ellie said. "My mommy makes pumpkin pies."

Present tense. Jolie caught the mistake instantly. But rather than tell the five-year-old that this wasn't the type of pumpkin with which one made pies, she smiled and said, "Yes. Your mom used to make the best pumpkin pie in the whole wide world."

She'd purposely used the past tense and waited for Ellie's reaction.

Thankfully there was little. Merely a downcast expression, her long, pale lashes resting against her flushed cheeks.

"So," Jolie ventured, crossing her arms and rounding the monster pumpkin. "What's the verdict? Do you think it will fit in the back of the Jeep?"

She asked the question only because she already knew the answer.

Ellie eyed the pumpkin, then the Jeep, then her gaze drifted back again while Jolie held her breath. Of course she knew what the logical answer was. But she had to remind herself that life through a five-year-old's eyes wasn't always quite so black and white. Especially after what had transpired in Ellie's in the past twenty-four hours.

"Sorry, gals." Old Man Peterson's voice boomed across the lot as he sauntered over toward them. "If you had your hearts set on that one, I'm afraid I'm going to have to break them. This here pumpkin is slated for carving at the traditional Old Orchard Halloween Party in the town circle tomorrow night."

Jolie's sigh was so deep she nearly had to rest against the pumpkin before taking in another. Ellie stared at the gnarled old man and backed up until she rammed into the front of Jolie's legs. Jolie braced her hands against the five-year-old, realizing that was the first time she'd actually allowed herself to touch her. She gave the slender shoulders a reassuring squeeze and introduced the two.

"Eleanor, huh?" Peterson asked. "They wouldn't happen to call you Ellie, now would they?"

The girl nodded, her eyes huge in her round face.

"Thought so. I had a horse named Ellie once. Big thing, she was. And the most ornery cuss I ever did know."

Jolie smiled at his attempt at small talk even as Ellie dove around her legs, using them as trees with which to hide herself as she peeked at the tall man.

She cleared her throat. "Are you sure we can't have this pumpkin, Mr. Peterson? We were both thinking it would look really nice in our front yard."

He clucked his tongue. "Very sure. Mayor Nelson put town money down on it himself clear back to last year. He wasn't happy when the Wentworths got the largest pumpkin then."

A familiar meow pulled Jolie's gaze toward the field just on the other side of the fence. She looked down to see Ellie was also watching Spot, who was circling a good, normal-size pumpkin, then rubbing against it affectionately.

"Is that Spot?" Old Man Peterson asked, scratching his chin. "I don't think I've ever seen her out this far. Means something important's about to happen."

Jolie frowned at him. She knew the rumors surrounding the cat's exploits. She was just surprised a man Peterson's age believed them. Didn't wisdom come with age?

"Sorry, Mr. Peterson, but I think Dusty and Ellie and I will be the proud recipients of whatever Spot has up her fur. She tagged along in the Jeep with us."

His rheumy green eyes seemed to twinkle as he looked at her and his grin was wide and full of mischief. "Yes…yes. I'd say if anyone was deserving of a miracle, it would be you three."

Jolie was jarred almost right out of her boots.

"Let's go see about the pumpkin Spot picked out for you, huh?"

Ellie took that as her cue and dodged around Jolie's legs, through the gate, then straight to the pumpkin Spot was now stretched out on top of, her long, black limbs tipped with white hanging over the sides.

Jolie stared at the feline for a long moment, her breath puffing out her cheeks before she exhaled. Then she shook her head and preceded Mr. Peterson into the patch.

Chapter 12

Dusty stood on the front porch, freshly scrubbed and in a clean pair of jeans and sweatshirt, a coffee cup cradled in his hands as Jolie's Jeep pulled into the drive. Even from here he could see that her face was drawn and tight, her constant furtive glances toward Ellie, who sat stalwartly staring out the window, telling him all had not gone well on their outing.

He swallowed hard, forcing himself to wait on the porch when he really wanted to walk to the car. He watched Jolie round the Jeep and open the passenger door, helping Ellie out. The five-year-old kept her eyes to the ground as she walked toward the house, then disappeared inside when Jolie opened the front door, the cat on her heels.

"Go ahead and hang your coat in the hall, sweetheart," Jolie called after her. "I'll be in in a minute to get you that snack we talked about."

Jolie softly closed the door, then collapsed against it. Dusty watched her face as she murmured something under her breath. She sighed, meeting his gaze for the first time since pulling into the drive.

"Didn't go as planned, huh?" he asked, longing to reach out and tuck a stray, windblown strand of hair from her flushed cheek.

"Oh, no, it went great. Fantastic, even." Her gaze grew wistful. "She was talking, Dusty. Conversing. Full sentences."

He frowned. "So then what happened?"

She pushed from the door and shrugged, absently taking his coffee cup from his hands and sipping from it. Her grimace told him she'd just discovered it was black. "Oh, Elva Mollenkopf happened. Right in the middle of town. We'd stopped at Old Jake's General Store to pick up some pumpkin-carving materials, and who should we run into while stopped at the only light in town? Elva."

He accepted his cup back, gazing at it as he tried to figure out exactly where her soft, full lips had been and feeling an intimacy he wasn't sure he wanted to be feeling just then.

Jolie waved a hand. "Of course she undid in one minute flat what had basically taken us twenty-four hours to do."

"What'd she say?"

"What didn't she say is more the appropriate

question. She told little Ellie she was sorry about the death of her mother, and what an awful way it was to go, one of the most awful deaths imaginable, but not to worry because her mommy was gone and couldn't feel pain anymore. And that maybe it would be best if her father just went ahead and died, too, because he was going to be so burned he would be looked upon as a freak, and how sad it was that she was now an orphan, just like Little Orphan Annie, without the red hair, and how she felt sorry for her because she was all alone in the world now."

She finally came up for air, the reiteration of the exchange coming out in one long rush and leaving Dusty as upset as Jolie must have been when Elva uttered the foul words.

Her voice dropped. "It was all I could do not to run the light to get away from Elva." She closed her eyes and shook her head, then walked to the opposite side of the porch, her back rigid and tense, her jeans clinging nicely to her bottom and legs. "I don't know. Why is it some people aren't happy unless they're making other people miserable?" She stuffed her hands into her pockets. "Ellie is only five years old, for God's sake. That alone should make her exempt from all adult manipulations."

Dusty put his cup down on the railing. "Maybe she went after Ellie because she's such an easy target," he suggested. "Or maybe she's completely clueless and has no idea what she said was so wounding."

Jolie shot him a glance over her shoulder.

He shrugged. "Or maybe not."

Jolie turned her head away again. Dusty glanced

toward the door, noting the silence from within the house and wondering what, if anything, little Ellie was doing. He opened the door and stepped inside. The five-year-old had turned on the TV and sat staring at the screen sightlessly. He stepped back out on to the porch and quietly closed the screen door.

"She was the first one to say something to me after you'd gone."

Dusty's gaze was drawn to the back of Jolie's head at her quietly said words.

"I thought...well, I'd assumed I'd have a couple days to myself, to get my thoughts together, figure out what I was going to say before I had to explain our circumstances to everyone. But my first five minutes outside and bam, there was Elva, telling me she was so very sorry you'd left, but wasn't it my fault, really, because any woman worth her salt should be capable of keeping her man. Then she went on to say it was probably for the best, because you and I weren't really suited for each other, anyway, and didn't I see that now."

A tight fist of frustration formed in Dusty's chest.

Jolie gave a brief, humorless laugh. "The funny thing is that I hadn't even told anyone that you'd left... *Really* left. I merely told them you'd gotten a good job in Toledo." She slowly shook her head. "But Elva knew. I don't know how, but she knew."

Dusty quietly stepped toward her, stopping mere inches away, the crisp autumn breeze bringing her subtle, irresistible scent to his nose. "I'm sorry."

"Don't be. You did what you had to." She cleared her throat. "It's funny, while Elva makes it very easy to pinpoint blame, it was shortly after she said what she had that I realized it wasn't that she was smarter than everyone else. It was that she was the only one willing to speak the truth. That no matter what I said, what I did, they all knew. Every last person knew you had left me." Her head tilted forward as she dropped her chin to her chest. "I was the only fool who thought you might come back."

Dusty was filled with the urge to touch her. To let her know without words what he was feeling. He wanted to tell her that he almost had come back. Countless times. Once he'd even climbed into his truck, driven the hour and a half to Old Orchard and spent an entire night sitting outside on the street watching the house, wanting to go in so badly it hurt.

But he hadn't gone in. He'd known that had he come back like that, nothing would have changed. That after a blazing honeymoon, the cycle would start back up, leaving him right back where he started.

Now he damned that pessimistic belief. It was so easy to come up with these great ideas when you were alone, when the other person involved wasn't in front of you, her shoulders trembling. So damn easy...

A car came up the street, then pulled into the driveway. Dusty's hand froze in midair and he noticed Jolie give a shiver, as if in anticipation of his touch. A car door slammed, followed by another, breaking the moment in two.

Dusty slowly took his hand back and cursed under his breath. Until he turned and saw his widowed sister-in-law, Darby, crossing the yard, her twin girls—Erick's girls—beside her.

* * *

Jolie felt Dusty's withdrawal and her heart twisted in her chest as Darby climbed the front steps, hugging her.

"I would have come sooner, but I had to run one of the animals out to the vet." She pulled away, then turned to hug Dusty. Only Dusty had backed up, gazing at his nieces as if unsure what to do.

Jolie's heart hiccupped.

Then the twins took the uncertainty right out of his hands as they rushed their uncle, each clutching a side of his hip with their skinny arms.

"Uncle Dusty!" Erin said.

"We've really missed you," Lindy added.

Jolie's throat grew tight with emotion as she watched Dusty instantly bend down and catch a twin in each arm and lift them off their feet, eliciting squeals of delight. "Not half as much as I've missed you." He kissed them both on the top of their tawny heads. He pulled back and looked at them, his eyes filled with a mixture of pride and sadness. "Is it, um, just my imagination, or have you two put on a couple pounds since the last time I've seen you?"

Lindy lifted her chin. "I've grown a whole inch since summer," she announced.

"Have not," Erin countered.

"Have, too."

"Have not."

Dusty lowered them one by one back to the porch, resting his large hands on top of their heads. "Let me see if I can help out here." He pretended to measure them, then heaved a huge sigh. "I don't know, Erin.

Looks like she might be just a tad taller than you." Jolie
bit her bottom lip to keep from smiling. As the firstborn,
Erin liked to pretend she was the larger, smarter and
faster of the two girls. And at her uncle's pronounce-
ment, she glowered. Dusty snatched her back up,
catching her unawares. "But don't worry, sweet pea.
You'll catch up in no time at all."

Darby smoothed back Lindy's hair. "Maybe. If she
eats all her vegetables like I ask instead of feeding them
to Arnold under the table."

"Arnold?" Dusty cocked a brow as he put the girl
down. "Don't tell me you still have that old porker."

"Yes, we do," Lindy confirmed with a serious nod of
her head. "Sheriff Sparks calls him Pork Chop. What do
you suppose he means, Uncle Dusty?"

Dusty met Jolie's eyes and her stomach flipped at the
teasing light in his. "Oh, it's just an endearment, Lindy.
Like sweet pea. And lamb chop. And sweetheart. And
princess." He crouched down and cuddled both girls
close again until they begged to be set free.

Darby stood next to Jolie, her arms crossed over her
chest, her eyes suspiciously moist.

Dusty got up. "Hey, I've got an idea. Why don't we
go inside and tell Ellie all about Arnold."

"Who's Ellie?" Erin asked.

Darby almost imperceptibly shook her head, indicating she hadn't told them.

"Oh, she's this little girl about your age who's
going to be staying with us for a while. Would you like
to meet her?"

"Yes," Lindy said.

"No," Erin objected.

Dusty chuckled good-naturedly and opened the screen door. "How about we find an answer that falls somewhere in the middle…"

His voice faded off as the threesome trotted inside the house.

Jolie smiled after them, a flush of relief and warm gratitude swirling through her veins like the colorful autumn leaves in the front yard.

Darby leaned against the railing next to her, apparently feeling a measure of that same relief. "God, for a minute there I was afraid he was going to run."

"Me, too," Jolie admitted quietly.

Darby turned her head, taking in Jolie's appearance, then smiling. "Well, don't you look good."

Jolie rolled her eyes and stared at her good friend. "Considering I just had a run-in with Elva Mollenkopf downtown, I'll take that as a compliment."

Darby's expression sobered. "Elva has a way of eclipsing even the sunniest day, doesn't she? Sometimes I wonder if Angela was right. The woman has to be a vampire."

Jolie jerked her head to look at Darby, her breath snatched away from her. "It's so peculiar you just said that. I saw…at the store the other day, I ran into Angela. Before…" She swallowed hard. "She saved me from Elva and said the exact same thing you just did." She briefly closed her eyes, then forced herself to exhale. "I still can't believe she's gone."

"Neither can I," Darby agreed.

They lapsed into silence and Jolie wondered how

much her sister-in-law was thinking about Erick's death, the gap in her own life that had been caused as a result.

Darby quietly cleared her throat. "You know, the day of Erick's funeral, Elva came up to me and said that it was better that he'd been taken from me now, while I was still young enough, pretty enough to find someone else." She gave a visible shiver. "I wanted to punch her." She moved her lips from side to side, thoughtfully. "At the time I couldn't imagine even wanting anyone else again." She shrugged down a little further into her coat. "I still can't."

Jolie quickly blinked her eyes.

"Speaking of funerals," Darby said quietly, looking at her. "You're not taking care of that, too, for Angela. Are you?"

Jolie shook her head. "No. The Old Orchard Women's Club is seeing to the arrangements. Something quiet. A brief memorial the day after tomorrow."

"I'm glad. Maybe I'll stop by this afternoon and see if there's anything I can do to help." She reached over and picked up a bag she'd brought with her. "I was going through a few of the girls' old things. God, can you believe I'm using the word *old* in conjunction with anything having to do with the girls?" She sighed. "Anyway, I thought maybe you could use some of it for Ellie."

Jolie accepted the bag. "Thanks." She glanced down inside, spotting a frilly purple something or other lying on top. She fingered it, then pulled the tiny scrap of material and lace out.

"It was Erin's Halloween costume last year." She frowned. "Well, almost costume. She wanted to be a ballerina until five minutes before we left the house for trick-or-treating and she changed her mind and went as Britney Spears. She never even wore it, except for fitting sessions. I thought…well with tomorrow being Halloween and all…I thought maybe Ellie might like to have it."

The shiny, stretchy fabric was so soft, so tiny, in Jolie's fingers, she found it amazing that the leotard could fit anything larger than a doll. She smiled, blinking back the sudden moisture flooding her eyes. "Thank you. I wasn't…I didn't know if I should get her anything. This way…well, you made the decision much easier for me. It means so much more what with the connection to you and the girls."

Darby draped an arm over her shoulders and squeezed. "Ah, the emotional roller coaster begins." She smiled warmly. "I swear I'll be in the middle of doing something as mundane as making one of the girl's beds, or folding their socks, and I'll just burst into tears."

Jolie laughed, the sound choked and soft.

Darby squeezed her shoulders again, laying her head against hers. "By the way, if I didn't tell you on the phone this morning, I just wanted to say that I think it's great. You know, what you and Dusty are doing for Ellie."

Jolie put the adorable costume back in the bag and set the bag by her feet. "I can't imagine not doing it."

"I'm not surprised to hear you say that."

Jolie wiped her damp cheeks with the back of her hand. "How are things going, anyway? Vampire Elva aside?"

She nodded. "They're…going. Ellie and I went out

and picked out a pumpkin at Old Man Peterson's patch a little while ago."

Darby groaned. "The girls and I went yesterday. Don't tell me, she wanted that monster pumpkin in front, didn't she?"

Jolie nodded.

Darby laughed in response.

Jolie lapsed easily into silence, happy just to enjoy the moment of peace with her friend. Bask in the unique bond that had always existed between them. As only children, their relationship was as close to sisterly as Jolie ever thought she'd get. Or believed she deserved. There wasn't a day that went by that she didn't thank God for having Darby in her life.

"Anyway, that's not what I meant when I asked how things are going," Darby said quietly.

Jolie pulled her head away to look at her, smoothing back her hair from where it had stuck to Darby's. "How do you mean?"

Darby crossed her arms, her eyes full of mischief. "I want to know how things are going between you and Dusty."

She felt her cheeks flame hotter than any fire she'd ever faced. "Ah."

"Yeah, ah," Darby said. "Come on. You can tell me."

Jolie stared down at her hands.

"Both you and I know you've got to talk to somebody, Jolie, or else you'll burst."

She cleared her throat. "I visited Gramps yesterday."

"Uh-uh. Doesn't count. The person you talk to has to be able to talk back."

"Ouch."

Darby shrugged. "If you had wanted tact, you would never have chosen me as a friend."

Jolie couldn't help a smile. "I guess hoping some of mine would rub off on you was too much to wish for."

"Uh-huh. Now give."

Jolie averted her gaze, unsure of what to tell her about her and Dusty. Unsure if there really was anything to tell. Despite their having given themselves over to temptation two days ago…sleeping on the couch together last night…the first snatches of real conversation they'd had since before Erick died…when all was said and done things stood the same between them. The divorce papers were still tucked under the knives in the silverware drawer, and Dusty still planned to leave.

"I wish there were something to tell you, Darb," she said quietly. "The truth is, I don't know how this thing is going to turn out. But if I had to wager a guess I'd have to say not good."

The teasing light vanished from her friend's eyes. "Do you want me to see what I can do? Try to knock some sense into him?"

Jolie smiled sadly. "No. If there's anything to be worked out, Dusty and I are the ones who are going to have to do it." She drew in a deep breath, then let it out. "Right now I'm just taking it one minute at a time."

"And?"

"And what?"

"What do you have planned beyond that?"

Jolie frowned at her, not sure she understood what she meant.

"Come on, Calbert, you have to have something planned. You know, some sort of seduction scheme to tempt him back into your life."

Jolie felt herself flush all over again. "I'm not the seductive type." Not that she needed to be, if the other day was anything to go by.

"Don't tell me you're just going to sit back and let him go?"

Jolie's throat tightened to the point of pain as she eyed her friend's shocked face. "If it comes down to that…yes, that's exactly what I'm going to do, Darby. I can't make him stay. Not without resolving whatever problems exist between us."

"The guy loves you, Jolie. Surely you have to know that."

She didn't have to know anything. But she did know that. "Maybe. But maybe that's not enough. Maybe that's something he needs to figure out by himself."

"With no help from you."

Jolie glanced toward the open front door, listening to the sounds coming from the direction of the kitchen. The peal of the twins' laughter, the clanking of something metal. Then Dusty shouted to them that lunch was on and that they'd best get in there unless they wanted a specially commissioned posse sent after them.

She caught herself smiling. "Well," she said quietly. "I wouldn't exactly say without *any* help from me."

Darby curved her arm over her shoulders again and laughed. "That's more like the Jolie Calbert Conrad I trained…er, remember."

Jolie slowly picked up the bag and led the way inside

the house, wondering if things could really be that easy. That if she decided to try to win Dusty back, she could. Just like an engine that needed some attention every now and again to keep it running smoothly, maybe all her and Dusty's marriage needed was a tune-up.

Her throat tightened and the smile left her face. Who was she kidding? Her relationship with Dusty needed an entire overhaul.

Chapter 13

Every time Dusty looked at his twin nieces, he felt as if his heart might burst. They were identical twins, but he'd never had a problem telling them apart. It all boiled down to what characteristics they had inherited from their father, his brother, beyond the blond hair and brown eyes. Erick's competitive spirit and mischievousness shone clearly in Erin's eyes, lending her an impishness that contrasted against her angelic features. On the other hand, Erick's lopsided, easy grin was apparent on Lindy's face, giving a quirky type of playfulness to her otherwise serene features.

Darby laughed at a particularly ribald joke Erin had just shared, though it was clear the six-year-old hadn't a clue what the punch line really meant. But Dusty's mind was on the person who was missing from the cheery lunch in the sun-filled kitchen. Erick.

His chest muscles contracted until it was difficult to breathe, and he felt he might suffocate if he didn't get air into his lungs, and fast. His gaze scampered around the room, from the half-filled soup bowls, the half-dozen casserole dishes he'd put out on the table, to the faces of those who inhabited the room. But no matter where he looked, he couldn't escape the panic spreading throughout his body and creeping up his neck.

Someone poked his arm. He absently looked down to see little Ellie hesitantly stabbing a pudgy finger into his bicep, her blue eyes huge and translucent.

Dusty finally took a needed breath and the panic threatening began to abate. He leaned down toward Ellie. "What can I do you for, El?"

She pointed at the jug of milk he'd placed on the corner of the table. He automatically reached for it.

"One refill coming right up," he said, pouring the white, frothy liquid into Ellie's empty glass.

He was aware of the twin's sharing a skeptical glance. Then Lindy shrugged and held out her glass. "Me, too, Uncle Dusty."

"Well, if she's going to have some, then I'd better, too," Erin said in amusing resignation, pushing her glass across the table in irritation.

Darby's eyes crinkled at the corners as she smiled. "You're a wise, wise girl, Ellie," she said. "Milk does a body good."

Erin crossed her arms and flopped back in her chair. "You say that now. Just wait for the ride back to the ranch when Lindy starts farting and stinks up the whole truck."

The room went silent for a telling moment, then Jolie burst out laughing.

Dusty found a grin breaking through as he watched Darby elbow Jolie. "Erin, what have I told you about using such words? Especially at the dinner table?"

The six-year-old grimaced. "Okay, then, when she passes gas. Or is flat…flat…"

"Flatulent."

"Yeah."

Dusty cocked a brow. "An awfully big word for such a little girl," he said.

"Flatulent," Ellie said, her first and sole contribution to the lunch conversation.

Laughter abounded anew.

In the corner, the telephone let out a sharp chirp. Dusty automatically began pulling from the table, realizing Jolie was doing the same at the opposite side. Their gazes met and he froze. It was then he grasped that it was no longer his place to answer the phone.

Jolie began reseating herself. "You go ahead," she said quietly.

"No, you really should get it."

Dusty was aware of Darby's telling frown as she watched the quiet byplay. "Would you like me to get it?" she asked finally at the third ring.

Dusty grinned at her. "Wouldn't you just love to know who's on the other end." He rounded the island and plucked the receiver from the cradle, ignoring what his immediately getting up to answer the phone, and Jolie's encouragement for him to do so, meant.

"Yeah," he said as casually as possible.

"Dusty? It's Jones. We got a four-alarm down on Main. The general store. Tell Jolie I need her. I need everybody we've got to help knock this one down. I could even use you."

Dusty's fingers tightened against the warm plastic. "I'll tell her."

A pause, then, "Good. Thanks."

Jones hung up, but Dusty stood for long moments, his fingers seemingly frozen to the receiver as Jones's words rushed through his mind then back again. *I could even use you....*

Dusty hauled the phone from his ear and slowly hung it up. He hadn't worked a fire since Erick's accident six months ago. Didn't even know if he had it in him anymore. He already knew he didn't have the stomach for it. He'd nearly bodily stopped Jolie from going into the Johansen's yesterday when all she'd been doing was her job.

"What is it?" Jolie asked from the table.

For a fraction of a moment he considered not telling her. But he knew he couldn't do that. Not wanting her to go and lying to her were two very different things.

His gaze flicked over the expectant faces staring at him. From the twins who were frowning at his unexplained silence, to Darby's apprehensive silence, to little Ellie, who'd dropped her chin to her chest while squeezing her napkin so tightly he thought it might disintegrate.

"Four-alarm down on Main." He decided not to tell everyone there that it was the general store. Fire was bad enough without associating it with someone or some-place you knew. "Jones needs you down there pronto."

As if on cue, the city siren calling volunteer firefighters to duty pierced the air outside the house.

The twins started to get up. Darby stayed them with a quick hand. "Oh, no you don't. You two just sit right where you are. This doesn't concern you."

"Aw, Mom..."

She gave them each a reprimanding stare, then glanced at Dusty. "Why don't you go down with Jolie. You know, so she won't have to leave her Jeep on the street. I'll look after Ellie." She glanced at the youngster who had yet to lift her head. "In fact, why don't the four of us just go on out to the ranch. I want to check on Julius after the vet visit. And maybe Ellie can help out with the afternoon feeding." She reached out and gently grasped the little girl's hands, stilling them. "What do you say, Ellie?"

Jolie was already standing, pulling on her jacket. "Boy, I'd rather do that, myself."

Dusty grimaced as he looked at her. He suspected there wasn't anything out there that Jolie would like to do better than fighting fires. Putting her life in danger. Charging in like some hell-bent heroine on a mission.

He rubbed the back of his neck. "Thanks, Darby. I think I'll do that."

Two hours later, every last one of Jolie's muscles screamed for relief. Despite the cool October temperatures, she sweated under the turnout suit. While physical exertion was the main culprit, working side by side with Dusty again after so long was just as much to blame.

She cast him a furtive glance as he helped her up on top of the roof of the general store, but he wasn't looking at her. Instead, his mouth was drawn tight, his face as tense as she'd ever seen it, and she spotted evidence of his own sweating across the handsome expanse of his forehead.

She motioned toward the far corner of the building. "Chief said we should reventilate over here."

He swept the beam of the flashlight over the area, spotlighting where the earlier ventilation had been made not too far from where they stood, then nodded. He grabbed her when she would have cut a diagonal path across the rooftop toward the area in question. "Stick to the sides," he said.

She nodded, skirting the one-foot rise at the edge of the building twice, then taking her ax from her pocket. She made an invisible cross with the blade, mentally marking where she wanted to hit, then froze, staring at Dusty's face.

Jolie dropped the ax to lie pick-first on the rooftop. "Are you okay, Dusty?"

His gaze flicked to hers and she drew a quick breath at the odd mixture of emotion she saw in the brown depths of his eyes. He seemed angry and hurt all at once. An unusual combination she didn't quite know how to react to.

Throughout the seven years they'd worked together before, he'd always been a go-getter, Johnny on the spot, refusing to let anyone else do something he was chomping at the bit to do.

However, she noticed that over the past two hours, he'd lagged behind, almost trying to make himself invisible, except when the wall downstairs caved in and they'd needed the extra hands.

His jaw tightened. He hadn't thought twice then. "I'm fine. Let's just get this over with so we can get out of here."

Jolie's heart skipped a beat at the sound of his voice. "Okay. Shine the light here."

He did as asked, standing slightly off to the side as she lifted the ax and pounded once, then twice, until the blade punctured the blacktop-and-tar tiles. Working the edge inside, she jimmied the material until a thin stream of smoke billowed out. Smoke caused by the dousing of the fire below. After a few more carefully aimed hacks, she judged the hole wide enough.

"That ought to do it," she said, dropping the ax to her side.

He nodded, then began walking back the way they'd come.

Jolie tried to ignore the way her heart thudded in her chest. While fixated on how Dusty was reacting to the experience, it was easy to ignore her own feelings. But now that the fire was under control and soon to be completely extinguished, she could no longer put off examining the peculiar emotions pulsing through her veins. It was almost as if for the first time she could see herself through someone else's eyes. While she'd been able to concentrate when the occasion called for it, always there, lingering on the edge of her consciousness, was Dusty's point of view.

For the first time she knew fear and trepidation, where before there had been none beyond the normal caution she exercised in her job. Nerves she didn't know she possessed now tingled with a sense of danger, of foreboding. Her chest hurt with it, her mouth was dry, and she felt almost sick to her stomach.

Is that how Dusty was feeling at that very moment? How he had felt since the moment he received the call from Jones? Was it how he felt whenever he watched her suit up, eager to go out on a run?

She dragged the back of her gloved hand against her forehead, pushing her bangs back out of her eyes. She wasn't sure she wanted to see herself through Dusty's eyes. Especially not now, when it appeared the decision to end their marriage had been made. She didn't want that kind of connection, understanding. The time for that had come and gone. Especially given the sober expression on Dusty's face.

"You go first."

Jolie started at the sound of Dusty's voice, eyeing where he was stopped at the side of the building in front of the iron fire escape. She nodded and did as he suggested.

When they were both back safely on the ground, and had apprised the chief of their success in reventilating, he gave them a thumbs-up.

"Good." Jones heaved a sigh and looked at his watch. "It looks like we have this baby knocked down. Why don't you two head on home. Group 2 can take care of things from here, see to the overhaul."

Jolie's throat tightened. *Home.*

And twenty minutes later, after the shucking of their turnout suits, a silent truck ride home, and a phone call to check up on Ellie, who was asleep at Darby's, that's exactly where they were. Home. Alone.

Jolie washed her hands in the kitchen sink, then scrubbed them with cleanser to get the soot out from under her fingernails. She absently wondered why it should seem funny to be alone with Dusty. Before they'd taken on care of Ellie, wasn't that how they'd been? Alone?

But somehow being alone with him now was more intense, more meaningful and decidedly more intimate.

"Why don't you take the first shower?" Dusty offered, shrugging out of his coat, then hanging it on a hanger on the back porch to air out. Jolie watched him make movements he'd made a hundred times before, but only now really registering them.

He closed the door and she shook her head, concentrating again on her nails. "No. You go on ahead. I'll catch one after you're done."

She felt his gaze on her face but refused to meet it.

"Are you sure?"

She nodded and bit her bottom lip as she held her hands under the streaming water. "Yeah." She smiled tremulously. "You know I always needed a few minutes to get my thoughts together after a fire."

He cleared his throat. "I'd forgotten."

What else have you forgotten, Dusty? The question zoomed through Jolie's mind, but she refused to ask it. Instead, she waited until she heard his footsteps on the stairs before switching off the faucet and absently wiping her hands on a kitchen towel. For long moments she stood like that, staring through the back window onto the lawn that needed cutting, the leaves that needed raking, and considering a relationship that was long overdue for attention.

She supposed that in the city, a couple like her and Dusty might seek out counseling to delve into the problems that plagued them. But here, in Old Orchard, they had to rely on themselves. A challenge she hadn't been up to. A challenge she feared she wasn't up to now.

How could she hope to help Dusty get beyond his fears if she didn't completely understand them? Yes, she may have gained a bit of insight into how he felt on the site, but she couldn't help thinking that was but the tip of the proverbial iceberg. And if he wouldn't share his feelings with her, any attempts she made to make things right between them, to heal wounds she couldn't see, would remain that: hopeless attempts.

She closed her eyes, listening as the shower switched on upstairs. Running her fingers over the rough material of the towel, she found the concept of Dusty completely nude, washing the dark soot from his muscular body, almost unbearably normal. And temptingly erotic.

She gave an involuntary shiver, trying to recall something her grandfather had told her once, when she'd burned the chicken for the fiftieth time and was about to give up on cooking altogether.

"Sometimes knowing isn't enough, Jolie C. Oftentimes you have to trust your instincts, stop looking at the clock, measuring the flame, and turn those pieces when you think it's time to turn them."

She'd been cooking from an old book she'd found stuffed in the attic, circa 1950, that included instructions down to the depth of the oil in the pan. The next time she made the chicken, she followed Gramps' advice and found he was right. She'd been paying so much attention to the details, she'd stopped listening to her instincts.

She popped open her eyes and laid the towel on the counter. Is that what she'd been doing with Dusty? Paying too much attention to what was wrong, and ignoring what was so right between them?

And if she were to try to listen to those instincts now, what would she find they were telling her?

She swallowed hard, knowing exactly what they were whispering. The heat covering her skin, the dampness between her thighs, and the pulsing of her body told her she wanted to go straight upstairs and climb right into that shower with Dusty. With her husband.

Chapter 14

Dusty turned his face into the undulating spray of the shower, but no matter what he did, he couldn't seem to shake the anxiety holding his muscles hostage.

What had happened to the guy who could boldly step into any fire situation without a second thought? Face down the red, licking monster without blinking? Follow a grueling day with a beer or two with the guys and shoot the breeze as if they'd done nothing more significant than yard work?

He leaned a hand against the shower stall and dropped his head, allowing the spray to cascade down into his face. That man, that Dusty Conrad, had disappeared along with his brother six months ago.

He stood like that for long minutes, under the punish-

ingly hot shower, trying to get a handle on his emotions.
Was Jolie right? Could his current behavior, his recent
decisions, be linked straight back to Erick's death?
Rather than her being to blame for their estrangement,
could he, in fact, be the one responsible for the loss of
the best thing in his life?

He shuddered despite the heat of the shower, then
turned around, wiping the moisture from his eyes. When
he opened them again, he found one very naked, very
proud Jolie edging her way into the shower, looking at
him expectantly.

Dusty groaned, wondering if he'd ever seen a more
welcome sight. "Hi," he said.

Her fleeting smile told him how lame his greeting
was. "Hi, yourself." She glanced down at where the
water swirled down the center drain. "I, um, decided I
couldn't wait. You know, for that shower."

He shifted slightly. "There's more than enough
room for two."

Her gaze flicked back up to his face. "Actually, all I
need is room for one."

She hesitantly reached out, her hands finding the
water-covered planes of his chest. Dusty's heart stut-
tered and he caught her fingers in his, examining the
sexy intent in her eyes.

God, how he wanted this woman. Had always wanted
her. And looking at her now, her hair slick and smooth
against her head, water droplets clinging to her lashes,
moisture running over her pink, full lips, he was as-
tounded he'd found the courage to leave her.

Or had it been courage? Had his fleeing from his

job…his home…his wife…been an act of cowardice? A result of the same fear he'd experienced on the fire site earlier?

"Please…kiss me, Dusty," Jolie whispered, whisking the water from her ripe flesh with a quick, anxious flick of her tongue.

He gently grasped her shoulders and turned her until she was leaning against the side of the shower, then lowered his mouth to hers, doing exactly as she asked. Doing exactly as he yearned to.

He slowly drew his tongue along the rim of her lips, dipping between them, intoxicated by the taste of the water and her own unique flavor. She made a sound in her throat and curved her arms around his waist, tugging him nearer, closer, until his hard flesh pressed against her softness, the heat of the water no match for the growing heat of their bodies. He gained access to the depths of her mouth, then dropped his hands to her breasts. Her shudder edged up his need for her even more as he plucked at her engorged nipples, rolling them between his fingertips, telling her with his body what he couldn't with words.

Sliding his tongue into the honeyed depths of her mouth, he reveled in the texture of her teeth, her warmth, her responsiveness, aware of her curving her leg around his, seeking a closer, more intimate contact. He slid his right hand from her breast and blindly reached for the soap in the stand behind her. Cupping the bar in his hand, he positioned it against the delicate line of her collarbone, then drew it down between her breasts, then up and under a firm mound, wondering at the pliancy of her slick flesh. Her own fingers dipped down to curve around his rear, then up the length of his back, her attentions suddenly restless as he drew the bar down to her belly button, then down even lower.

Jolie tugged her mouth from his, dragging in deep gasps of air as he slid the soap between her swollen folds, drawing it back...and forth...then back again.

"Oh, yes," she murmured, kissing his shoulder, then taking his skin between her teeth.

He drew the soap out, then moved it down one slender hip and thigh, bringing it up under her arm then over, repeating his movements until every inch of her skin was covered with lather, until not a whiff of the acrid smell from the fire remained, only the scent of the soap and one-hundred-percent pure, hot Jolie.

Her fingers trembling, she took the soap from him, apparently intent on doing the same to him. Her gaze caught and held his as she slowly, torturously budged the solid bar along the planes of his chest, over his flat, hard nipples, down over his abs, then teasingly bypassed the area in most need of her sensual ministrations, instead circling his waist and drawing the bar along his back.

Dusty thought he would die from anticipation as he fought to hold as still as possible, to allow Jolie the room she needed to explore. He clenched his jaw and hissed when her hands again flitted across the hypersensitive skin of his lower abdomen. Then she lathered her hands and placed the soap back into the dish and plunged down to the area that had been longing for her attention the most.

The feel of her sudsy, slippery fingers curving around

his pulsing erection caused him to groan in barely suppressed longing. But suppress it he did, his mind spinning, his skin burning as she stroked him lengthwise, then circled his arousal and squeezed. Dusty realized he had his eyes clamped shut and cracked them open, watching Jolie's wonderfully expressive face through the steam. Her attention was on what she was doing, her tongue dipping out to lick her lips as her hands continued their skillful stroking.

The rush of blood toward Dusty's groin warned of his impending climax. He thrust his hand to still hers, holding her gaze when she blinked up to look into his eyes.

"Darlin', the next step I'd rather have us do together."

She took in a deep breath, the move inflating her chest, and bringing her wet breasts into sensual relief. He bent briefly to nuzzle them, to drag her hot, hard nipples deep into his mouth, then he cupped her under one knee and moved her to rest against the side of the shower stall.

Finally his rock-hard erection pressed against her slick, swollen, ready flesh. Dusty knew a moment of hesitation. Not because he didn't want her with all that he was. Not because he sensed second thoughts from her. No. He wanted to savor the moment. Commit to memory the pounding of the shower spray against the porcelain tile. The sound of Jolie's ragged breathing echoing in the small enclosure. The feel of her moist folds against him.

He slowly bent his head and claimed her mouth. As his tongue slid against hers, as her sweet smell filled his nose, her hands restlessly explored his chest, then circled around to draw him even closer. He knew he'd never experienced a moment more exquisite. Genuine. Honest.

When they were apart, the outside world intruded, life allowed him the opportunity to consider those things that pointed to a lack of commitment. But when they were together like this…on the verge of lovemaking…their hearts hammering a rhythm only the other understood, he knew that what they had was unique. Precious. There was no room for pettiness. Only honesty, pure and simple.

And pure and simply, he loved Jolie Calbert Conrad with all his heart.

Jolie tilted her head back and whimpered low in her throat. Dusty positioned himself and thrust deeply into her hot, tight flesh. An intense shudder surged up from his feet to his neck, leaving not a muscle untouched. He slowly withdrew and plunged again, breathing in her shallow moan and cupping her face in his other hand.

He was unprepared when she lifted her other leg to curve it around his waist, and he adjusted, moving until both hands cupped her bottom, supporting her weight against the wall with his hands and body. He'd barely recovered when she tilted her hips forward, taking him deeper, farther, than he could have on his own. He stretched his neck back and groaned, knowing there was nowhere on earth that he'd rather be in that moment. Knowing that the heaven he was exploring with Jolie was the only matter of importance.

When he thrust into her sweet, welcoming flesh again, he did so with growing urgency, undeniable need, his mouth following his body's lead and deepening their kiss. Wet skin smacked against wet skin, feeding his passion until he shattered into pieces as small and as light as the droplets pelting them. Jolie cried out his name and tangled her fingers in his damp hair, her own climax freeing him in a way he couldn't comprehend, could only sense.

Two days ago their coming together had been urgent, intense, quick, their minds filled with confusion and doubt. Now they had joined with complete understanding of what they were doing, what it meant, and with full knowledge of the significance. That, alone, filled Dusty with a hope he hadn't thought he was capable of feeling again. The same hope that had filled him the day he realized she was the woman he wanted to marry. And the day of their wedding, when he'd lifted her veil to find her blue eyes shining at him full of love.

Drawing air deep into his lungs, he closed his eyes and rested his face against her neck, reveling in the pounding of her pulse there. His hands still supported her. Her stomach moved against his as she fought to catch her own breath, find her own way back from the stratosphere with whatever knowledge she had gained from their lovemaking in order to apply it to the here and now.

He swallowed when he felt her press her lips against his temple, then again to his cheek, her trembling hands gently holding the back of his head.

He smiled against her sweet-smelling skin. "I finished the Jacuzzi this morning." He drew back, searching her emotion-filled eyes, gazing at her swollen, well-kissed lips. "You want to try it out?"

Her mouth slowly widened in a lazy smile filled with mischief and desire. "Lead the way."

He carefully disentangled her legs from around his waist and lowered her, helping her to stand on the tile. She switched off the water even as he pushed open the shower door, white clouds swelling out to fill the cooler outer bathroom with steam. Steam caused as much by the hot water as by their even hotter lovemaking.

Dusty took a fluffy navy-blue towel from a nearby pile and leisurely draped it over her shoulders, using a soft corner to tenderly wipe the moisture from her forehead and cheeks. She blinked up to look at him, as if sensing he had changed, had come to some sort of conclusion, and his actions were portraying them.

"Jolie, I—"

The ringing of the telephone in the bedroom cut into his words. He blinked, refusing to allow the sound to intrude, intent on continuing. Determined to tell her that he didn't know what tomorrow held, but that he wanted them to figure it out…together. But the sound of the town fire alarm exactly on the second ring of the phone sliced into his warm intentions as cleanly as a fire ax.

The light in Jolie's eyes dimmed and she blinked, pulling the towel more tightly around herself.

"Leave it," Dusty found himself asking softly.

He watched her throat work around a swallow and her gaze move to somewhere beyond his shoulder.

"I…I can't," she whispered. "I just…can't."

She moved to pass him and he gripped her shoulders. "You can't…or you won't?"

Confusion, sadness and determination filled her

eyes as surely as passion had only minutes before. "That's not fair."

"Isn't it?" he asked roughly, his voice quiet. Too quiet. "Well, tell me, Jolie. Is it fair for me to have to play second fiddle to your career? A career that rips you away from me when I need you most? A career that leaves me wondering whether or not I'll still have a wife at the end of the shift? Or whether or not I'll be attending another funeral?"

The shock on her face was undeniable. "I…"

Dusty grabbed another towel from the pile. "Never mind, Jolie. Answer the phone."

Chapter 15

Jolie sat in the passenger's side of Dusty's truck, feeling raw, exposed and torn in two. Her muscles were still pleasantly sated and clamoring for more, compelling her to want to tell Dusty to stop the truck, head back to the house, forget about the fire and climb into that big, hot Jacuzzi with him to take up where they'd left off. Literally, and figuratively. Both in their lovemaking…and their marriage.

She couldn't be exactly sure why, but something in Dusty's eyes after they'd made love in the shower had made her heart skip a beat. It was as if he'd come to a conclusion about her, about them, about their marriage, and nowhere was the fatalism she'd grown accustomed to seeing. Instead, lurking there in the depths of his rich brown eyes, she saw love. Clear and bright. And she felt warmed by it all over. It made her remember how tender he could be, how loving. Inspired in her a longing for the way things used to be. No, no…not like how they used to be. Better.

Next to her, Dusty cursed under his breath and made a turn too quickly, the rear truck tires squealing against asphalt. Jolie turned to stare out the passenger window, considering the other side of the coin.

While having glimpsed the love in his eyes made her yearn to stay home with him, to explore all that was right between them…having him ask her to stay was quite another thing altogether. Especially since she sensed his request hadn't been merely a genuine desire for them to continue what they had so innocently started. Rather the sudden hardness in his eyes hinted at a more important, and ultimately more urgent motive.

Jolie absently rubbed her forehead, willing away the tension there. Didn't Dusty understand? Firefighting was her job. When the phone rang, when the siren went off, she had to go. Yes, after the fire earlier in the night, she had gained some insight into Dusty's feelings. But did that mean she had to change hers? She felt a desire…a need to fight fires that she couldn't hope to explain. She supposed part of the reason harkened back to the loss of her own parents. But it was more than that. So much more. She reveled in the powerful feeling of battling something larger than herself. Basked in the camaraderie that existed between her and her fellow firefighters that was as much a part of the station as the engine. Was humbled by the reminder that life was fleeting and she needed to grasp onto it with both hands.

She stared down at her hands now, finding them clasped tightly in her lap. Of course, she feared her attempts to hold on to Dusty had ultimately failed. It was a fear that spread through her bloodstream along with the adrenaline she always felt before a run.

"Sweet mercy…"

Jolie glanced at Dusty, his words softly spoken. He'd taken his foot from the gas, and as the truck slowed, he stared through the windshield at something that put his striking features into warm relief. Jolie's throat tightened as she slowly followed his gaze. They sat on Old Orchard near Main…the perfect vantage point to see that nearly the entire downtown was ablaze.

"Oh, my God," she whispered, her hand going to the front of her throat.

On the phone, Jones had mentioned something about Devil's Night, typically the night before Halloween when street gangs and restless teens set fire to abandoned homes. Jolie's emotions had been in such turmoil, the big-city term hadn't registered with her. But it did now.

Only Devil's Night was what happened in larger cities, wasn't it? Smaller towns like Old Orchard were immune. They didn't even have street gangs. Did they? It was well-known that in Detroit, only a few hours away by car, the night before Halloween proved the busiest for area firefighters. But never in the history of Old Orchard had they had to worry.

Never…until now.

Dusty pulled the truck to a stop at the curb and

climbed from it as if in a daze. Jolie followed suit on the other side, gripping the truck door to anchor herself against her churning thoughts, the heat of the fire hitting her skin like the sun after a particularly cold night.

The fire they'd knocked down at Old Jake's General Store had rekindled. And an assessing gaze told her it was perhaps the source that had ignited the businesses surrounding it, given the amount of damage and the hot orange flames lapping through the broken front windows. The general store. Eddie's Pub. The Old Orchard Public Library. All lay victim to the growling fire, setting the whole east side of the street aglow, while the other side sat eerily silent, awash in the ominous yellow light.

Jolie shivered, absently leaving the truck door open as she started stepping toward the closest fire truck, then lengthened her strides until she was nearly running. She was vaguely aware of Dusty doing the same beside her.

She'd never faced anything near the proportions of this fire. Stood before a blaze eating nearly an entire city block filled with places she'd frequented her entire life. Businesses that had names, and friendly owners, and were chock-full of memories for her.

"What's the status?" she heard Dusty ask Sal.

Sal wiped his hand across his soot-covered face as he closed a valve on a reserve tank and opened another discharge line, the edgy energy emanating from him as intense as the fire. "Just what it looks like. We covered the store fire, headed back to the station, then got called back a half hour later." He was shaking his head, his hands working on automatic as he stared at the consuming blaze. "The damn thing was knocked down. I was sure of it. Not even an overlooked hot spot could have done this. Had I overlooked one. Which I didn't. In the two minutes it took us to get here, the pub and the library were already under. A half hour later, this...."

Jolie glanced to find Dusty squeezing Sal's shoulder. Not that the veteran firefighter noticed. She recognized the signs of shock. But so long as he continued working his way through it, he would be fine.

Chucking her jacket, Jolie rounded the truck and reached in the cab for the extra turnout suit, her gaze on the lookout for the chief, who would be directing the scene from somewhere centrally. Her nose was already filled with the smell of charred wood, her mind with the reality of ruined lives.

There. There was Chief Gary Jones. In front of the demolished general store, speaking into his radio. Even he was covered in soot, indicating that he'd gone into the fire himself.

"Is there an extra one in there?" a voice asked from behind her, the familiar sound sending shivers up and down her spine.

A moment later, Dusty came up from behind. Jolie continued pulling the bunker pants up and drew the suspenders over her shoulders, then blinked to find Dusty standing next to her. Swallowing past her tight throat, she reached in the cab, then handed him the last extra suit and pair of boots. She left her shoes on as she stuffed her own feet into the too-large boots. Gathering the coat, hat, mask and oxygen supply, she started off toward the chief. She noticed that Old Man Peterson and the temporary pastor, Jonas Noble, were approaching from the opposite direction.

Gary finished issuing an order to ventilate the east side of the library roof, then rubbed his face, further smearing the soot there.

"Chief?" Jolie asked.

He glanced at her, the soot making his lined face seem even more ancient. "Three weeks from retirement and I get the worst fire of my career." He turned to stare into the raging blaze. "My God, it seems like everything that is Old Orchard is on fire."

A couple of more men stepped from the shadows. Jolie recognized them both and nodded. Not that the chief realized they were there. His eyes were a million miles away as he stared into the licking flames.

"Where do you want me, Chief?" she asked, shrugging into her coat. Hands grasped hers. She looked up to find Dusty offering to help her secure her air cylinder. She searched his eyes, looking for any sign of what had passed between them back at the house. The tenderness. The passion. The love.

There was none.

The chief strode toward the front of his Jeep, where a rough diagram of the block had been laid out and on which he was keeping track of the assault.

"Martinez and Holden just came out of the pub after the north portion of the second floor collapsed. I need someone to get back in there to stop the fire from spreading to Smyth's dry cleaners next door as soon as the first team beats back the frontal flames." He glanced at her, then Dusty. "Can you two handle it?"

Jolie glanced at Dusty. His face was rigidly calm. Too calm. Could he handle it?

Dusty's heart slammed against the wall of his chest in ominous, even pulses, pumping blood and adrenaline and fear throughout his body.

"Can you two handle it?" he heard Fire Chief Jones ask.

Dusty noticed the question in Jolie's wide eyes, then with barely a second thought, he nodded. "We got it, Gary."

The chief looked instantly relieved. "Good. Now, I need…"

Dusty tuned out because Gary was no longer talking to them. He'd turned his attention to Peterson and the pastor and the other men, leaving him and Jolie staring at each other.

Jolie didn't have to speak. He could see the words swimming in the depths of her eyes, eyes made black by the eerie shadows cast by the fire. She was wondering if he was up for this. Remembering how he had choked earlier in the day, while they were ventilating the roof of the general store. Now, as then, seeing the doubt made his gut twist, his pulse pound harder. Not because of the fear he felt. But because Jolie didn't trust him.

She averted her gaze and stuffed her hands into her gloves, then lifted her hood and her helmet to her head. "I'm going on over to see how far along they are."

Dusty nodded, distractedly securing his suspenders, then shrugging into his coat as he watched her walk away until she disappeared around another truck. Damn. Never in his life had he seen in Jolie's eyes what he'd just seen now. She'd always looked at him as if he were some sort of hero, larger than life, a man capable of anything and afraid of nothing.

How did he tell her that his new take on life, on her, stemmed from his fear of losing her?

Dusty began to turn back toward the chief when a familiar figure caught his attention. As he fastened his hat and shouldered his pack, he squinted at Scott Wahl. He wasn't surprised to see the teenager there. The way he'd taken to hanging out at the fire station, he was probably one of the first on the scene.

Securing his jacket, he stepped toward the teen.

"Scooter?" he said, wondering what he was doing there standing alone and not insisting he be included in the fire-fighting activities. Hell, given the scope of the blaze, the chief probably would have put him in.

An ominous cracking sounded from in front of them.

"Heads up!" John Sparks called, having traded his sheriff's uniform for full turnout gear. Sparks motioned for others to get back. A moment later, the awning over the general store gave way, crashing to the wide sidewalk in a cloud of red sparks.

Scott stumbled back a couple of steps and shook his head. "It's so…big."

Dusty glanced at the storefronts stretched out before them. "That it is."

A pungent curse caused him to glance behind him. He found Sal shaking his hand, likely having injured himself while keeping on top of the gates. Using his other hand, he finished tightening a valve, then called out, "Tank's at ten!" The truck's built-in water tank was down to ten percent capacity. That meant the narrower attack hoses would be useless in a few minutes. A visual sweep found the two hydrants at opposite ends of the streets being utilized by the crews at full power. "Where's Lee City Fire Department with the extra tank, damn it?" Sal swore.

Dusty clasped a hand on Scott's shoulder. The teen jumped and stared at him through wide, terror-filled eyes.

"Standing here watching is only going to make things worse," Dusty said quietly, feeling the urge to reassure the kid. He gestured over his shoulder with his thumb. "Why don't you go see how you can help Sal? I'm sure he'd appreciate it. And the activity will take your mind off things."

Scott nodded almost imperceptibly, then slowly began moving in Sal's direction. Dusty watched him for a long moment, wondering if Scott had been cured of the firefighting bug. Or whether this was a momentary setback caused by the enormity of the blaze.

He tucked his chin into his chest and headed toward where Jolie waited for him. Across the street, he noticed Mrs. Noonan was setting up shop in Penelope Moon's New Age store. Somehow all the women were acting as if it was the middle of a perfectly normal Sunday afternoon for a church social, rather than the disaster-in-the-making it was. Mrs. Noonan and her Old Orchard Women's Club had set up tables with the help of Penelope's lights. Mrs. Noonan was putting out disposable cups full of beverages, while even Elva Mollenkopf was making sandwiches, cutting the crusts from them, and arranging them on a tray. Dusty watched as one of the firefighters swooped by the table and grasped a half sandwich and a cup of coffee, then swung back to the front line.

Dusty aimed his gaze in front of him, seeing Josh and Joe McCreary, two brothers who sat way in the back of the church every Sunday, who mumbled whenever you asked them how they were doing, and generally acted as if they wanted to be anywhere but there. Yet here they were, the first ones in line when somebody needed help.

Dusty spotted Jolie motioning for him in front of the second truck.

Here it goes…

He put one boot in front of the other. While he'd never worked a fire anywhere but Old Orchard, he couldn't see a neighborhood or a larger town pulling together the way they did in Old Orchard. No. Instead, there would probably be a group of spectators gathered on the street corner, pointing and talking. Here, no one was just standing, pointing and talking. Each and every one of them found a way to help any way they could.

"Are you ready?"

Dusty blinked, bringing Jolie's masked face into focus. Behind the safety glass, her mouth blocked by the vents and breathing tube, her eyes took on a surreal quality. Made him remember how beautiful they were. And how full of determination Jolie was.

He responded by pulling on his hood, his mask, checking the airflow on his air cylinder, then flicking on his mike, which had a feed straight to Jolie and the chief. They performed a test to make sure the radios were working, then he passed her and led the way into the burning building.

* * *

An hour later, Jolie stumbled from the door of the pub, her air cylinder dangerously low, exhaustion pulling at her limbs. She felt as if she was walking through mud as she concentrated on putting one foot in front of the other until she was far enough away to pull off her mask and take in gulping breaths of air.

She was aware of Dusty behind her, but could focus on little more than her own breathing, dropping her mask and hat to the ground and supporting herself by resting her hands on her knees. Once her heartbeat started to slow, she glanced up to find Dusty standing in front of her, his hat tucked under one arm, looking as if he was ready to go into the fire instead of having just come out of it. He didn't appear in the least bit winded. His back was strong and straight. His face serious and unsmiling as he stared at the thick smoke still billowing through the broken windows. But thank God there were no flames.

Jolie's heart gave a tight squeeze.

His gaze rested on her as she straightened. "Are you all right?" he asked.

She nodded, pushing her hair back from where it had escaped the clip at the nape of her neck. "I will be."

The chief rushed up, another man at his side, more than likely the commander from the neighboring town's teams. "Good job, you two. At least we won't have to worry about the fire spreading to the dry cleaners."

Jolie turned toward the flames still devouring four of the buildings on the other side.

For the past fifty minutes, she and Dusty and a couple of other firefighters who'd joined them later, had worked side by side, fighting back the fire that threatened to engulf the entire building and move onto the one next to it. They'd stacked up debris, broken all the windows, taken down flammable material, then doused the pile until not one spark remained.

"Here."

Jolie glanced to find someone holding out a small water bottle. She followed the hand up to stare into the face of Elva Mollenkopf.

She slowly accepted the bottle and murmured a quiet thanks, but irrationally refused to drink from it until she watched Dusty nearly down the contents of his bottle in one breath. He finished, then ran the back of his hand across his mouth, his brown eyes twinkling at her. "What's the matter? You think she might have poisoned it?"

Jolie grimaced and glanced at her watch. "I suppose it's safe. It's not officially Halloween yet."

Dusty's soft chuckle made her smile as she sipped from the water, welcoming the cool liquid against her parched mouth and throat.

A figure stepped out from inside the little that remained of the general store. Jolie realized it was John Sparks and he was holding two severely melted plastic containers. He put them down near the chief, then pushed off his helmet and mask. "I found these in the back room of Jake's place."

Jolie looked closer. "What are they?"

"Ten-gallon gasoline containers."

Her gaze shot to his.

"That's right. Looks like all our suspicions are correct and that we may have an arsonist in our midst."

Dusty took off his air cylinder, then slipped out of his

coat. "Well, at least we can be thankful they targeted the fire during a time when foot and customer traffic was light. No one got hurt."

Chief Jones sighed. "Almost no one. Pastor Noble got pinned down by a bookcase at the library. Think he busted his leg."

Jolie frowned. An arsonist? She remembered her line of thought earlier about Devil's Night and all it entailed. Was it possible a group of teens had started this fire? But in other cities, abandoned homes on the demolition list were usually the targets. There was no mistaking that this stretch of Main Street was far from abandoned.

Gary scratched the top of his head. "That would certainly explain how the sucker rekindled after we performed the overhaul."

A voice crackled over the radio. Gary stepped a foot away to respond.

Jolie dropped a shoulder and let the strap of the air cylinder slide down her arm, doing the same on the other side. She lowered the canister to the ground, then straightened her jacket, feeling more tired than she could remember ever feeling.

"Maximus! Max, get back here now!"

Jolie turned toward the voice, finding Penelope Moon calling her dog. She clapped her hands, but the mixed breed of setter and Great Dane barked, then playfully avoided the owner in the middle of the street.

"I'll get him!" Scott Wahl called out, stepping from where he was helping Sal at the pumper.

"Oh, God," Jolie whispered, an arctic chill inching up her spine.

Just as she feared, the dog, caught between Penelope and Scott, playfully darted first one way, then the next, then figured out the only clear route for escape was behind him. And behind him lay the fire.

"Max!" Penelope's voice took on a more urgent edge as the dog barked, dodging water lines and firefighters, then ducking straight through the door to the pub from which flames still licked outside the upper broken windows, despite the full stream of water targeted at them.

Jolie immediately reached for her helmet.

"Oh, God," Dusty murmured next to her, shrugging into his coat.

She looked up in time to see Scott darting inside the building after the dog.

Dusty took off at a full run, Jolie right on his heels. They reached the front of the pub, only to be pushed back by a wave of heat as fire flashed inside. Martinez stumbled out, hauling his mask from his face and gasping for air. "She's going to blow!"

Jolie looked at Dusty and he looked at her. That the establishment stocked liquor went without saying. And the fact that liquor was incredibly flammable needed no mention, either.

"Where's Scooter!" Dusty grabbed the firefighter by the front of his turnout coat.

"Who?" He shook his head. "I didn't see anyone in there, man. My partner went through the back, and it's just as bad there."

Dusty pulled his mask over his face and Jolie did

the same with hers. He glanced at her, his eyes filled
with question.

She merely nodded.

And then he led the way into the building.

Chapter 16

Without the aid of an air cylinder, Dusty was forced to keep as close to the floor as possible. The area behind the bar where Eddie kept the hard liquor burned bright as day, the heat shattering bottles, the alcoholic contents of those bottles further feeding the flame.

His heart slamming against his chest, he tried to call out over the roar of the fire, but it seemed his words went no further than his mouth. He coughed and inched along the floor.

He knew the layout of the pub well. Just like most food or beverage establishments, the front section was open, with a long bar along the left wall with stools, and tables dotting the rest of the area. In the back was a jukebox and a pool table. Beyond that were the rest rooms and the storage room.

Glancing over his shoulder, he found Jolie on his heels, slowly scanning the area to her right and left. She looked at him and shook her head.

"I don't see him," she said over the radio.

Where was the dog? Dusty wanted to know. Surely after rushing inside, the mutt figured out that the game was over. Why hadn't he run back outside?

Dusty's foot caught on the leg of a chair and he kicked it out of the way, continuing his forward movement.

"The bathrooms," Jolie said. "Maybe he's in one of the bathrooms."

Dusty nodded. The men's room was to the left and some fifteen feet ahead. He started in that direction first, ducking when another bottle exploded, shooting off a wild flame.

"You guys near the bar?" a voice sounded through Dusty's earpiece. Martinez, he thought.

"No," he heard Jolie answer.

A moment later, a full stream of water, followed by another, was aimed for the ceiling above the bar, cooling drops raining down over the dancing flames with canny precision as their fellow firefighters hit the blaze with everything they had.

Dusty continued his forward movement, the low crouching position placing strain on his knees. He hadn't realized how quickly he'd gotten out of shape, despite his physical work in construction.

"Dusty, wait."

He heard Jolie's voice at the same time he felt her gloved hand on the back of his leg. He glanced at her over his shoulder. She was looking at something to the right, then she pointed, indicating he should look, as well.

Dusty swallowed hard, wondering if he was going to like what he was about to see.

He did as she asked, scanning the area by the pool table thoroughly. He couldn't see a thing. Jolie tapped on his leg again, motioning for him to move back a little. He did. And immediately spotted a figure crouched under the pool table, his back to them, his arms tightly holding the dog.

Jolie coughed, a deep, racking sound that reminded Dusty that she'd just suffered from major smoke inhalation the day before.

"Jolie," he said into the radio connecting them. "I can handle this. You go ahead and get out."

She shook her head. "You need help."

"No. I need you to get out of here before it's you I'm forced to help."

"Jolie," another voice sounded over the radio. This time Gary's. "Dusty's right. Come on out. Sparks says he'll go in to help."

Dusty met her wide, determined eyes. "Either you go, or we both go," he told her resolutely. "You decide. Which will it be, Jolie?"

Her mouth moved, but without her mike switched on, he couldn't hear what she was saying. When she started backtracking, he decided it was probably better that he hadn't heard her. He'd lay ten-to-one odds that the words weren't pleasant.

Smiling to himself, he turned back around toward the pool table.

* * *

Jolie emerged from the pub's doorway, dry, hacking coughs racking her body. Sparks stepped forward and tried to help her walk to the perimeter of the scene. Jolie waved him away. "Get in there!" she told him. "He needs help."

Sparks nodded and began moving back toward the building. Doubling over, Jolie rested her hands against her knees, slowly inhaling, then exhaling, trying to cleanse her lungs of the acrid smoke that filled them.

A loud blast vibrated the air, nearly blowing her back onto the street. The draft caught Sparks and sent him reeling toward a truck. Jolie stared wide-eyed as great, spurting flames arced through the open door to the pub, then were sucked back in again.

Oh, God, no! she cried silently.

She stumbled a couple of steps forward, ignoring the heat searing her skin. *No...no...no...*

Her eyes were glued to the front of the building as the firefighters in charge of the hoses retargeted their streams on the door.

"Wait! I see something!" Sparks shouted, holding his side as he started forward.

Jolie heard a bark, then Max leapt from the door, his fur soot-covered and matted, his pink tongue lolling out of his mouth as he ran toward his owner.

"Dusty?" she whispered, moving slowly forward. *Come on, baby, you can do it,* she silently told him. *Just find the door....*

Even as she mentally said the words, her mind was working through all the possibilities. First was that Scott was in a state of shock, and given his awkward position wedged under the pool table it would be very difficult indeed to pull him out. Second…

She shuddered, not wanting to acknowledge the other possibility. The chance that Dusty caught the brunt of the blast and was even now lying unconscious on the pub floor where he would fall victim to the toxic smoke.

Come on, Dusty, she said, continuing her silent mantra. *You can do it. Just get up. Pull yourself out if you have to. Just come back to me. Do you hear me, Dusty? Come back to me….*

She was near the door herself now, barely aware of where Sparks had caught up with her and had placed restraining hands on her shoulders. She absently tried to shake him off, trying to continue her forward movement.

Then, as if the fire itself had belched him out, Dusty appeared in the doorway like a black knight, Scott's body propped alongside his, the teen's arm draped over Dusty's shoulder.

Jolie thought she might pass out right then and there, her relief was so great, so all-consuming. As soon as Sparks had taken Scott, Jolie launched herself into Dusty's arms, nearly sending him sprawling back inside the door to the pub.

"Whoa," he murmured, taking off his helmet. "What did I do to deserve that?"

Jolie held him tight, her cheek pressed against the heavy, soot-covered material of his jacket. "You came back."

* * *

Dawn's purple fingers inched across the eastern sky, casting dim light over the charred remains of Main Street. Dusty stood in the middle of the street, feeling strange as he stared at the black, hollowed-out structures before him. If not for the tint of the coming sunrise, he could have been looking at a black-and-white photograph. The fire had claimed, eaten, destroyed every last bit of color, leaving nothing but monochrome skeletons in its wake.

They'd finally knocked down the monster two hours ago. Since then, every man and woman on the site had inched through the debris, soaking it, overhauling it, so that this time absolutely no hot spots remained. The job finished, everyone stood at various, random spots on the street, robbed of words as they stared at what night had hidden.

Old Orchard would never be the same again, Dusty thought, running his hand over his hair. Sure, they would rebuild. But gone was the century-old library with its faded brick foundation and stone roof. The general store that had served as gossip central as well as providing food and necessities was unrecognizable. The pub was destroyed, along with several other buildings, their naked walls reaching up three stories to touch the sky.

"Happy Halloween," Sparks murmured, slowly moving toward one of the silent fire trucks and stripping out of his coat.

Dusty absently watched him, then scanned the rest of the street, taking in the shocked, still faces of the men and women who had helped equally to try to preserve Old Orchard in her hour of need.

Chief Gary Jones sidled up beside him. "Maybe it will look better after we've all had a bit of sleep."

Dusty frowned. He didn't think it would ever look better. And the knowledge seeped down into his bones, finding a home there.

Gary scratched his head. "Look, I've got the bulldozers coming in an hour. You mind hanging around and helping me oversee the demolition?"

Dusty's gaze trailed down the opposite side of the street until he spotted Jolie. She was standing ramrod straight, her helmet in hand, staring at the altered town skyline. As if sensing his gaze on her, she looked his way.

Gary said, "I need the rest of the guys at the station. You know, in case, Lord forbid, something else happens and they're needed."

Dusty cleared his throat and broke eye contact with Jolie. "I'll stick around."

Gary thumped him on the back. "Good. Good."

Then he walked away, leaving Dusty alone again. He was vaguely aware of Jolie heading his way, but he didn't look at her. He was exhausted, stressed, and just plain confused. Their brief discussion after they made love in the shower seemed like days ago rather than hours. But no matter the time factor, his feelings remained the same. He'd asked her to stay with him. She had rejected him. It didn't matter that Old Orchard was in the middle of the worst disaster in her history. All he'd needed Jolie to do was nod. Say she would do anything for him. Then they could have gone together. But she hadn't stayed. Had barely even hesitated before letting him know exactly where he stood in her heart. And that was dead last.

She came to stand in front of him. He kept his gaze stalwartly on the rubble.

"What did Gary want?" she asked quietly.

Dusty finally lowered his gaze, taking in the streaks of ash across her forehead, the blue of her eyes, the soot covering her hair. God, he loved her more than anything else in the world. If only she could love him back in the same way. "He asked me to hang around, help with the demolition. I told him I would."

She nodded. He half expected her to say she'd stay, as well. Instead, she turned back toward the debris. Penelope Moon's dog Max was sniffing around the edges, but he didn't make a sound. It was as if he, too, understood the significance of what had happened there.

"I just talked to Darby," Jolie said. "She's bringing Ellie by the house in an hour. I think someone should be there. I should be there."

Dusty stared down at his boots. "Yes, you should."

"So," she said slowly. "I guess I'll catch a ride home with Sal, then."

He didn't say anything.

"I'll see you back at the house in a couple hours?" Her words were hesitant, soft.

Dusty wanted to tell her no. That he wouldn't be going there again. Instead, he found himself nodding. There was still the matter of the papers. And little Ellie. This time he would do things right. Leave no doubt as to his intentions. When he left this time, it would be for good. "I'll see you back at the house," he said, then turned and walked away, leaving her standing by herself in the middle of the street.

Chapter 17

The following evening, Jolie adjusted the tiny tutu on the even tinier ballerina leotard, then gently turned Ellie around to face her. They were in the middle of the second bedroom, which no longer resembled the guest room, with the aid of Jolie's careful ministrations and Darby's helping hand. Ellie might have been staying there for weeks rather than three days. She'd even named all the stuffed animals and the doll the twins had given her and stacked them just so against the wall, one on top of the other. Jolie couldn't help thinking the five-year-old's rekindled interest in the life surrounding her was a good, healing sign.

Jolie tapped a finger against her lips, restraining a smile as she took in the precious little girl in front of her. "I don't know…"

Ellie's frown was almost comical. "What's wrong?"

Jolie shook her head. "I don't know…" She sat back on her ankles and pretended to scrutinize the adorable costume, when in reality she was committing every last detail to memory. The way the neckline scooped to reveal her defined collarbone, the hand-stitched lace edging that made it more a costume than a regular leotard. She tugged on the tutu. "Turn around for me. Yes…like that. All the way."

Even the white tights and satin slippers were divine. Jolie's throat tightened with emotion. She remembered her own mother fussing over her when she was no older than Ellie was. Now she understood the funny expressions her mother used to wear.

Ellie shifted impatiently from one foot to the other.

Jolie smiled so wide her face hurt. "It's…how do I say it? You're…absolutely, positively…perfect."

Ellie's return smile outshone even the sun setting outside the window. "Good enough for the party?"

"Party? Oh, you're talking about the annual town get-together." She placed her hands on Ellie's slender hips. "I don't know if they're going to have it this year, honey."

The five-year-old sucked in her lower lip, then released it. "But Erin and Lindy said they're going to be there."

A voice from the doorway caught their attention. "I just spoke with Gary," Dusty said. "The party's still on. The site's cleaned up, and the mayor thinks the towns-folk need to see what happened. To adjust."

"As if we weren't all down there last night," Jolie said quietly. She told Ellie to get her jacket, something light, just enough to ward off the slight chill of the night.

The five-year-old didn't move. Instead, she was looking at Dusty expectantly. Then it hit Jolie. She was waiting for some sort of response to her costume.

Jolie cleared her throat, vying for Dusty's attention and nodding her head toward Ellie. When he frowned, not catching on, she mouthed the words "the costume."

While he didn't say "oh," it was written all over his face as he pushed off the doorjamb. "My goodness, who do we have here?" he said, rounding the preening little girl. "Jolie, why didn't you tell me we were going to get a visit from a ballerina tonight?"

Ellie rose up on the tip of her toes, cupping her hands over her mouth. Dusty leaned down and the girl said loud enough for Jolie to hear, "It's me, Dusty. It's Ellie."

He pulled back, feigning shock. "Ellie? No…it can't be." He brought his face closer to hers, looking, and causing the girl to giggle. "Well, I'll be. It *is* Ellie."

Jolie rolled her eyes toward the ceiling, then held her hand out for Ellie's. "Come on. We want to be the first ones on the block to go trick-or-treating, remember?"

Ellie eagerly put her fingers in hers, then grabbed Dusty's hand, as well. Dusty's gaze lifted to Jolie's. Her stomach dropped to somewhere in the vicinity of her knees. And the feel-good emotions wending through her bloodstream seemed to evaporate, suddenly leaving her edgy and nervous.

Earlier in the day, when she'd returned home from the fire site, and stood in the same shower in which she and Dusty had shared so much the night before, she'd fallen completely to pieces. She'd tried blaming it on the stress of the situation, the long hours spent battling a fire that had destroyed so much, but she recognized the lies for what they were. She knew she was on the verge of losing Dusty forever and her heart had begun grieving. A state of mourning she refused to give herself over to for Ellie's sake.

But after Darby and she had shared a cup of coffee, and her sister-in-law left to go back out to the ranch, Jolie's mind kept returning to Dusty. Especially when he didn't come back until she and Ellie were having lunch at the picnic table in the back yard, both laughing at Spot as she chased a squirrel around in the fallen leaves, then up the old oak tree.

Dusty wanted her to quit the department....

Jolie had waited for the unfairness of his request to strike her. Expected her spine to snap straight, her ire to rise. But she'd felt nothing. Merely an aching pain in her chest that seemed to grow in intensity as each minute passed; as she remembered every empty minute of the past six months. Dusty had left her alone. And the department hadn't come near to filling the hole left in his wake.

She'd drawn a deep breath while watching Ellie play with a couple of neighbor kids in the backyard that morning, and questioned why being a part of the department in the first place had meant so much to her. She thought back to the god-awful loss of her parents...the purpose she'd felt after that...the need to battle a fierce animal that struck without prejudice, uncaring of who it killed, or who it left behind to fend for themselves in a world void of love.

But then she'd found love, hadn't she? She'd found it in Dusty's generous smile, his skillful hands, his comforting arms. Knew what it was like to be held, to understand that no matter what, that person was there for you.

Only in the end, she hadn't been there for him, had she? When Erick died, Dusty had needed her in a way he'd never needed her before. And she'd been so wrapped up in her own life, her own problems, her own need to undo the bad that had happened with Erick's death and replace it with good, that she'd missed the signs that her marriage was in trouble.

But after last night…

Jolie shivered and took a deep breath, feeling both free and so full of pain her body throbbed. Dusty was right. She'd been living her life fire to fire. Looking beyond what she had in front of her and searching for something that couldn't be found outside, but only from within: acceptance of her parents' deaths. Acceptance of Dusty's love. And his demand that she quit the department was his attempt to get her to see that.

"Jolie?"

Dusty's voice broke into her thoughts and she turned her head toward him. Slowly she focused on the bedroom surrounding her, grew aware of the tiny hand tightly clasping hers, and she managed a tremulous smile.

"Jolie, we're going to be late," Ellie complained.

Jolie met Dusty's gaze, thinking the five-year-old's words all too on par. Only it wasn't merely getting late. Seeing the distance in Dusty's brown eyes told her it already was too late.

Dusty returned to the house later that evening, alone. He placed Ellie's overflowing pumpkin-treat holder on the kitchen table, his eyes catching on a familiar sheaf of papers neatly folded and propped on top of the gleaming wood. Suddenly numb, he pulled out a chair and sank into it.

That explained why Jolie had suggested he not stick around for the town's annual Halloween party. He'd thought she might not want to confuse everyone by being seen together. Instead, she had been setting up the scene he now faced.

He picked up the papers and tapped them against the table. He didn't need to look. He already knew they were signed. But rather than the relief he had expected, instead he felt a pain so cutting, he didn't think he could get up from the chair if he'd tried.

He closed his eyes and swallowed hard. *Damn it, Jolie,* he thought vehemently. *Why did you do it?*

He came to realize something about himself in that moment. He saw that while all his actions had led up to this very point—his leaving, his returning, his attempts to force them both to get on with their lives, separately—he'd never really believed it would happen. Somewhere deep inside, he'd thought Jolie would fight his attempts to the end. That ultimately, somehow, some way, they would find their way back to the love that had always joined them together.

Instead, she'd given up.

His every muscle contracting, he glanced around the kitchen he'd spent his whole life in. But rather than seeing the memories of himself and Erick as he had been recently, his mind was filled with images of him and Jolie. Of the breakfasts they'd shared together. The long, leisurely discussions over steaming cups of tea. The late-night snacks that more often times than not had led to other, hotter late-night activities.

He turned his head toward the back window, to the yard beyond, and the town all around. Old Orchard. Home. He hadn't known how important the place was until he'd been forced to defend it when he'd sworn he'd never pick up another hose. Or when he saw the sheer delight on his twin nieces' young faces, so like their father that the grief he still felt over his brother's death had led to joy that he had these two important reminders in his life.

Despite the papers he crumpled in his hands, he realized he didn't want to leave there again. He'd already lost Jolie. He didn't want to lose the town, too.

He also found that in defending the town, putting on all his old gear, that he'd learned how to master his fear again. He ruled it instead of it ruling him. And while he didn't think he wanted to go back to firefighting full-time—the prospect of rebuilding Old Orchard appealed to him more—the thought of conducting training at the academy, or filling in part-time at the station, made him look at his future in a different light.

He only wished he could shine that same light on his marriage.

Dusty pressed the pads of his index finger and thumb against his closed eyelids, then rubbed, considering the debris that was his life with Jolie. Only fire wasn't to blame in this case. Not the way it was to blame for the destruction of so much of downtown. Oh, no. He'd played a dangerous, high-stakes hand of life poker with his marriage by trying to force Jolie into being something she wasn't…and he had come up the loser.

Something brushed against his ankle. For a long moment, he didn't respond, then the chair gave a squeak as he leaned back and looked down at the black-and-white scrap of fur vying for his attention. The cat looked back at him.

"What is it, Spot?" he asked dully. "Do you want to go outside?"

The feline circled his ankle again then meowed.

Pushing himself to his feet, Dusty strode to the back door and opened it. Spot merely stared at him.

"Well, go on, if that's what you want to do."

Another meow, but the cat stood her ground.

Dusty frowned and closed the door. He knew she couldn't be hungry because Jolie had fed her only an hour and a half ago. He headed back to the table, but Spot seemed to have other ideas as she brushed against his leg, as if trying to guide him away from the table and toward the hall.

Dusty stopped and stared down at the new addition to the household. "What? Do you want to be let out the front?"

A louder meow and a sprint toward the kitchen door gave him the uncanny feeling that the feline understood him.

Sighing, he headed in that direction. "Don't feel up to walking around, huh? You'd better watch it, fur ball, or you'll end up on a diet. Especially given the way you eat."

He opened the front door, then the screen door beyond, and Spot happily trotted through, stopping in the middle of the porch and twitching her tail. Dusty shook his head and began to close the door when he spotted someone sitting on the steps. The hair on the back of his neck stood on edge as he eyed the young man he'd mistaken for Erick once before. That Scott Wahl was sitting in his brother's old spot helped that illusion along.

"Scooter?"

The boy didn't answer.

Dusty stepped out onto the porch and allowed the screen door to slap quietly shut. Still, the teen showed no sign that he'd heard him. He walked to the steps, descended a couple, then dropped down to sit next to him.

"Scott?" he said.

Finally the teen glanced at him, a faraway, haunted shadow in his eyes, his skin noticeably pale under the glow of the porch light. Dusty squinted at him. The fire last night must have affected the kid far more than even he'd suspected. Which wasn't surprising. After a guy stared death straight in the face, he tended to look at life a little differently afterward.

Dusty cleared his throat. "Why aren't you at the party downtown?"

Scott shrugged, then leaned back on his hands, much in the way Erick used to. Only he wasn't Erick. Something was very evidently bothering Scott. Nothing ever seemed to bother Erick. His brother was always grinning, joshing and teasing…even in the moments right before his death.

Dusty looked down to find himself clasping his hands between his knees. Just like he used to. Only he wasn't that same guy from years ago, either.

For long minutes, he didn't say anything. And neither did Scott. The street was quiet. Unnaturally so, because the majority of the neighbors were downtown bobbing for apples, touring through the two haunted houses— one for adults, another for children—and enjoying the treats the Women's Club always supplied. Jolie would be there now. With little Ellie. Smiling and laughing.

Dusty absently rubbed his chest where a dull ache echoed there.

Spot bounded onto the bottom stair, nearly startling him. He absently petted the cat's head and glanced at Scott again. "You want to tell me what's on your mind?"

While it wasn't unusual for neighbors to visit one another in Old Orchard, Dusty could count the times he'd found Scott Wahl sitting on his steps on one finger. That it was Halloween, and he wasn't at the town cele- brations, or hanging out with his friends, or even at the station, made the situation even more curious.

"I bet you're thinking about the fire last night," he said quietly, turning to stare at the street in front of him, hoping the absence of his gaze would make the teen feel more comfortable. When he saw Scott jerk to look at him, he felt justified.

But still Scott said nothing.

Dusty nodded, sensing he had the teen's attention. "It was quite some fire. The worst I've ever seen, and I was with the department for a long time. I've knocked down a lot of fires. But this one…" He grimaced. "It's enough to strike fear in the bravest of souls."

He took a chance and glanced at Scott, hoping his words had laid the groundwork for the kid to open up.

But he glanced away, and while he couldn't be sure in the dim light, he thought Scott had blushed.

"It's okay to be afraid, Scott," he said, convinced that the incident with the dog, when Dusty had had to pull the teen out of the pub from where he was crouched under the pool table, was what was behind the kid's somber mood. Was the reason he'd even come to the house in the first place.

When Scott finally spoke, it surprised Dusty. "Do you think they'll put me in jail for a long time?"

Dusty cocked his head to the side, trying to make sense out of his words. "Why would they put you in prison, Scott?"

The teenager looked all of twelve years old as he dropped his chin to his chest. "I didn't mean for…all that to happen, you know? I just wanted to be given a chance. To prove to everyone that I had what it took to be a firefighter. No. Not just a firefighter—a great firefighter." He leaned forward, suddenly radiating nervous energy. "My brothers were always teasing me. Putting me down. Telling me I didn't have what it took. My girlfriend…Shawna…she laughed at me, said I was more of a station mascot than a real fireman and that I should get a real job."

Dusty remained silent, allowing Scott to work through his thoughts, although an alarm began chiming in the back of his mind. A four-alarm bell that the teenager was about to tell him something he wasn't sure he wanted to hear.

Scott looked at him dead on. "Those gasoline containers that John, I mean Sheriff Sparks found? I…"

His voice cracked and his shoulders slumped. "I put them there."

Dusty went completely still.

He recalled putting out the fire at the general store earlier in the day. Chief Gary Jones's certainty that they had completely knocked the fire down, leaving not a single hot spot behind. Scott's standing in the middle of the street, staring at the fire in wide-eyed shock.

He rubbed his hand over his face. He'd thought the kid's reaction was due to the enormity of the blaze. It had been. In a way. But only because he was the one who had restarted it.

Oh, my God.

Dusty sat there for a long moment, working everything out in his mind, glad that Scott lapsed into silence next to him.

"So," he finally said, looking at the teenager, careful to keep his face neutral. "What are you planning on doing about all this?"

Scott blinked at him. "I don't know."

Dusty took in a deep, calming breath, thinking of the catastrophic destruction of nearly half of Old Orchard's history. Then he reminded himself that the future of a young man's life was more important. Yes, the kid had done wrong. Yes, he should be punished. But that Scott realized what he did was wrong, that he was here offering up a confession…well, maybe all wasn't lost.

Scott shifted next to him. "Do you think I should go tell John…I mean, Sheriff Sparks?"

Dusty looked at him, then lightly draped his arm over the teen's shoulders. "Yes, Scott, I think we should."

* * *

The following afternoon, Jolie tightly gripped the Jeep's steering wheel, then released it. She felt both lighter…and heavier. Lighter because she'd just lunched with Nancy Pollard and had finally come clean on her and Dusty's situation. Rather than hear the words she'd feared, that Ellie would be removed from their custody immediately, Nancy had smiled and shared some news of her own. The child psychologist was very pleased with the progress Ellie was making, the bond she was forming with Jolie, and despite the uncertain nature of Jolie and Dusty's relationship, would she consider keeping Ellie for the duration of time it took her father to recover? Alone, if need be?

Jolie tucked her hair behind her ear, finding her hand shaking as she did so. Of course she'd agreed. After talking with Nancy for two straight hours, she'd also put in an official request to foster other children…with the hope of adopting.

The traffic light ahead of her turned red. She pulled the Jeep to a stop. The town circle sat before her, all cleaned up from the Halloween festivities the night before, the arcs of water the fountain sprayed up reflecting the midday sun's rays. Jolie's gaze moved beyond the fountain, gazing at the empty lots across the way on Main Street. Her stomach dipped as she stared, stunned, at all the destruction. And to know that little Scooter Wahl had been the cause of it… She shook the thought from her mind, having too much to think about without adding the boy's uncertain fate on top of the others. She was glad that Dusty had stepped forward, agreeing to act as Scott's guardian until his case came up for trial. With Dusty on his side, and the rest of the fire department, she knew that the teen would get the help he needed.

The light changed and she drove the short few blocks to the house. As it always did in the past few days, her throat tightened at the sight of Dusty's truck in the driveway.

When she'd come home last night, she'd found the papers gone from the kitchen table, and Dusty noticeably missing. She'd checked the master bath, only to find everything done, though she took little pleasure in seeing the gleaming tiles, the monstrous Jacuzzi installed and working. All she could think about was what had passed between her and Dusty the night before last in that very room.

She'd found out later that he'd walked Scott to John Sparks's, where the remorseful teenager had confessed to setting the second fire at the general store. But that hadn't stopped the acute pain that resided in her heart, making it almost impossible to breathe at times.

Flicking on the blinker, she pulled up into the drive beside Dusty's truck. Movement caught her eye. She glanced at the house to find Dusty coming out. Her pulse speeded up when she spotted the duffel bag he held.

He's leaving.

Of course, she knew he would. But knowing and being prepared were two completely different things.

Her limbs growing numb, she forced herself to get out of the Jeep, to walk on the brick path still blanketed with leaves, then to climb the steps. Finally, she stood on the porch...and felt as if her heart would beat straight through her chest.

She couldn't bring herself to look at him.

He cleared his throat. "I...I, um, didn't want to go without saying goodbye."

She nodded, as if she understood, but right now understanding was the farthest thing from her mind.

"I'm not going back to Toledo," he said quietly.

Jolie's gaze flicked to his face.

He grimaced. "I mean, I'll have to go back to close up my apartment, put in my resignation. But I plan to return to Old Orchard."

Return to Old Orchard...but not to her. Jolie's throat tightened so much she was afraid she might choke.

"I just thought you should know that. You know, in case we run into each other every now and again."

Every now and again...

She forced herself to nod, afraid to say the words on the tip of her tongue, afraid that the sob behind them might come rolling out, as well. Instead, she looked absently at the front porch swing, the red-and-white Ohio State Buckeyes stadium blanket lying across it. "And Ellie?" she asked.

He shifted from foot to foot. "She's inside. I explained everything as best I could."

She nodded again, then ordered herself to stop.

He moved toward the stairs and Jolie nearly cried out, wanted desperately to ask him not to leave. Her chest felt like it might cave in on itself.

"Goodbye, Jolie."

Then he was descending the stairs, getting into his truck

and driving away. And Jolie stood cemented to the spot, feeling like her world had just crashed to a sudden halt.

The door squeaked open, barely catching her attention.

"Jolie?" Ellie said quietly.

Glad the girl couldn't see her face, she covertly wiped the dampness from her cheeks, then turned to face her.

"*Scooby-Doo's* on."

A strangled laugh escaped her throat. *Scooby-Doo*. She smiled sadly, then grasped the door handle and let herself in. Maybe *Scooby-Doo,* and little Ellie, were just what the doctor ordered.

Chapter 18

Jolie sat in the office at the firehouse, going over the schedule for the next month. Eyeing the calendar, she paged backward, then forward, her gaze resting on the date. *December 1.* She ran her hand slowly down the page. It was hard to believe that a month had passed since Dusty had last said goodbye. Some days it felt like yesterday. Others, it seemed like years had gone by.

She dropped her hand to the desktop, trying to figure out what today felt like.

"Jolie, Jolie, I'm done! Do you think my daddy will like it?"

Busy, Jolie thought, filling in the gap. Today felt busy. Nothing more, nothing less.

She glanced up to where Ellie was bounding into the

office from where she'd been in the station kitchen drawing along with the rest of the guys. She got up to round the desk, nearly tripping over Spot. She frowned down at the cat. Somehow, the feline seemed a little more antsy today than she'd been recently. While her visits to the house were becoming fewer and farther between than they had a month ago, the fact that she stuck around the house at all, then was nearly on top of her whenever she was at the station, was puzzling.

Stepping around the desk, Jolie refused to buy into any of the stories that surrounded Spot's visits to her neighbors and the things that had happened as a result.

She gazed down at little Ellie, knowing the energetic, fun-loving five-year-old was to credit for giving her reason to be happy at all. She considered the picture Ellie had painted that would be tacked up with the half-dozen others she'd already made for her father on the hospital room wall.

She curved her hand under Ellie's chin and smiled. "I know he's going to love it, sweetie."

Two weeks ago Nancy had finally rubber-stamped the idea of Ellie visiting Jeff in the hospital. Up until that point, social services and the child psychologist had thought it would be too traumatic for Ellie to see her father in such poor condition. But after several trips to a Cleveland burn clinic for extensive skin graphs and reconstructive surgery, he had steadily improved and was progressing even more aggressively now that Jolie took Ellie by to visit him as often as she could. And if she couldn't do it, Darby did, generously filling in gaps that might otherwise have been handled by family members that Jolie didn't have. Of course, it also meant she looked after the twins on occasion, but she was coming to find that the fuller her house, the happier she was.

Yes, she would be the first to admit that being around others helped her ignore the pain caused by Dusty's final leaving. But it also aided the healing process. She found it awfully difficult to wallow in self-pity when a five-year-old was standing in front of her, footprints trailing after her, covered from head to toe in the mud she had dug up in the backyard, telling her she'd invited her entire kindergarten class for lunch.

And if every now and again her heart surged with hope that she'd spot Dusty whenever she ran errands or traveled back and forth to the firehouse…well, that was only natural, wasn't it? Just because things were over between them didn't mean he hadn't played a huge role in her life at one point. And she was coming to see that no matter how hard she tried, she couldn't make herself stop loving him.

"Are we going now? Are we?" Ellie asked, repeating herself in that eager way she'd taken to over the past couple of days.

Jolie grasped her shoulders and turned her around toward the hall. "Yes, we are. Go get your coat."

She watched the girl skip out of the office and close the door, then shook her head. Ah, to be that young and carefree again.

"What do you want, Spot?" she quietly asked the cat, who wound around her ankles again and meowed. "Sometimes I wish you could talk so you could just be out with it."

She patted the purring feline on the head, then turned and gathered her purse from the bottom desk drawer. There was a brief knock on the glass of the door.

"Ellie?" she called. "You can come on in, honey—"

Whatever words she might have uttered caught and held in her throat. Simply because when she opened the door, she found that Ellie hadn't been the one knocking. Dusty had.

Jolie's knees threatened to give out from under her. She blinked several times, just to make sure she wasn't seeing things.

No, she definitely wasn't. If she couldn't tell by looking at the strikingly handsome man in front of her, her complete physical reaction would have been a dead giveaway.

He stood in the hall wearing a well-worn pair of jeans, a black T-shirt and a leather bomber jacket. His brown hair had grown out slightly, making her remember how he'd looked before he'd joined the department, when his thick, wavy hair used to fall over his brow.

He looked good enough to eat. Either with or without a spoon.

"Honey?" he asked, hiking a dark brow.

Jolie opened her mouth to speak, to tell him that she'd been talking to Ellie, but nothing came out. So she clamped it shut again.

"Dusty! Dusty!" Ellie cried, catapulting herself down the hall and into his arms, crinkling the picture she'd drawn for her father between them.

He hoisted her up and took a good look at her, his grin nothing but one-hundred-percent irresistible.

"How are you doing, munchkin?" he asked.

Jolie knew that while he hadn't stopped by the house to see Ellie, he visited her often out at Darby's place. She also knew his visits meant the world to the little girl, who cooed about Dusty having said this, or having mentioned that whenever she saw him. If the new arrangement confused Ellie, she didn't say anything. Then again, after all that had happened in her young life, a little confusion was the least of her problems.

Dusty finally placed Ellie back onto her feet. Jolie gently rested her hand on top of her head, reveling in the feel of her silken hair against her skin.

She looked down at her. "Ellie, why don't you go into the kitchen and get the cookies we made for your daddy last night? That is, if the guys haven't eaten them already."

Ellie poked out her chin. "They better not have."

She started walking, then skipping down the hall. If her skip was a little lighter, a little happier, Jolie pretended not to notice. And that had nothing to do with the sudden skipping of her heartbeat.

She cleared her throat. "I hear the new construction company is doing well."

His gaze seemed to intensify as he scanned her face. "Yes, it is."

She nodded, her mouth feeling dry as dirt. "That's good."

For long moments she stood there, waiting for him to say something, to indicate why he was there, what he wanted. Only as an afterthought did she glance down the hall. She saw three adult heads and one child head duck back into the kitchen.

"So…" Dusty began, nodding toward the door where her name was painted on the opaque glass. "It's Chief Conrad now, is it?"

Feeling her cheeks heat, she looked down at her civilian clothes of jeans and a sweater, this being her official day off. She'd just stopped by the station to go over a few things before moving on to the hospital with Ellie.

"Yes, I am," she said, then stopped.

How did she explain to him that what he'd said to her before he'd left made a lot of sense? That the night of the Devil's Night fires, she had decided that she no longer had anything to prove on the front line and had decided on a compromise? To take the chief's exam at the same time she had her physical and claim the position Gary Jones had vacated only a week ago? But that she hadn't shared her decision with him because she'd thought it was too late?

She didn't know how to explain it to him, so she didn't. She merely smiled and said, "Not that I had any competition. Gary said that if I hadn't stepped forward, he probably would have been stuck here until they could bring someone in from outside." She shrugged. "I took pity on him and let him keep his hunting plans."

Dusty's grin made her curl her toes inside her hiking boots.

She swallowed hard, catching movement from the corner of her eye, but helpless to order the guys and Ellie to stop spying, and too distracted to invite Dusty into the office.

"So…" she began this time. "What brings you by the station?"

He slid his hands into his front jeans pockets and shrugged slightly. "I, um, was thinking of coming back part-time. Or being put on call, you know, in case you need an extra pair of hands."

"Here?" she asked. "At the station?"

His grin made a comeback. "Yeah. I meant to stop by before now, but I was waiting until things at the company settled down first." He cleared his throat. "The truth is, I've missed everybody here."

She turned, catching every last pair of eyes peering at them before heads were pulled back into the kitchen. She gestured toward their audience. "And obviously, they've missed you."

Silence fell between them, and Dusty's eyes grew darker. "I missed you, Jolie."

Jolie's stomach dove down to her ankles then back up again. She didn't know what she expected him to say, was at a complete loss for his reason for being there. But it would have been the last thing on the list, had she made one.

She didn't know how to respond. She pushed her hair behind her ear and tried for a smile. "Yeah, I've missed you, too."

They stood like that for a long moment, neither of them moving, neither of them saying anything. Then Dusty appeared to remember something. Moving his hand behind him, he slipped something out of his back pocket. Jolie instantly recognized the divorce papers…and she felt the sudden urge to run.

Dusty scraped his fingertip along the edge of the folded papers. "You know, when I went in the house to find these waiting on the kitchen table for me that night, I came to a ridiculous realization."

Jolie stared at his boots, unable to look into his eyes.

"I recognized that despite everything we'd gone through, even after I'd left, I never really thought it was over between us."

Her gaze flicked up to his face. "Dusty—"

"Wait. Let me finish." He ran his free hand through his hair and grimaced. "I don't know. I guess I took for granted your tenacity, your determination to see things through, no matter what." His swallow echoed in the hall. "And I realized that never in a million years had I expected you to sign these papers."

Jolie's breath caught. She tried to figure out where he was going with this, what he was trying to say.

"What I mean is…oh, well, hell, Jolie. I don't know what the right way is to say this…."

"Just say it, man," echoed a voice from down the hall.

Jolie glanced toward her colleagues, then back at Dusty, her eyes wide, her heart beating a million miles a minute.

She forced the words from her tight throat. "John's right. Just say it, Dusty."

The hopeful, unsure look in his eyes made her knees go weak all over again.

"I love you, Jolie." He dragged in a deep breath, then exhaled, laughing quietly. "There, I said it. I love you, have always loved you, and will continue to love you until the day I die."

"I love you, too," she whispered, her chest tight.

He didn't appear to hear her as he looked down at the papers he still held. "I…I never thought you'd actually sign these." He glanced at her from under his brows. "And didn't realize until the other day that despite what I'd thought, you hadn't signed them, had you?"

Jolie's cheeks blazed fire hot as she watched him unfold the sheets of paper, then hold up the page in question. He raised a brow. "Scooby-Doo?"

Just like that Jolie was in his arms, holding him as hard as she dared, filling her nose with the sweet smell of him, providing her starved body with the feel of him.

Behind her back, she heard him rip the papers in two, then his hands rested against the back of her head, gently tugging her until she was staring up into his emotion-filled face.

"God, woman, do you have any idea what you do to me?" he ground out, dipping his head to kiss her.

Jolie leaned against him for support, suddenly incapable of the simple task of holding herself upright as he slowly plundered her mouth. She ran her hands up his leather-covered back, then tunneled her fingers into his soft hair.

"Marry me," he said between fresh assaults on her lips. "Marry me all over again, Jolie. This time forever."

A soft sound escaped her throat as she burrowed closer against him, seeking his warmth, his love, his nearness. "Yes," she breathed.

A deafening, simultaneous whoop went up in the kitchen, at the same time the fire bell rang. But Jolie didn't even open her eyes. Didn't budge a muscle.

"Uh, Chief?" She heard Martinez call to her as the sound of the rest of the men scrambling for position filled the hall.

Jolie reluctantly tugged her mouth from Dusty's, laying her temple against his chin as she glanced at the fireman.

"It's the Glick farm again. Seems some teenagers were playing some pranks and let all of the chickens out this morning."

Jolie quietly laughed. "Well, then, you're just going to have to go out and help round them up, aren't you?"

Martinez grinned. "And you?"

And her? She glanced up at Dusty, finding passion and desire shining in his Irish-coffee-colored eyes. "After a swing by the hospital, then out to Darby's to drop Ellie off for a visit…my husband and I are going home."

* * * * *

Fall in Love with...

MEN
in UNIFORM

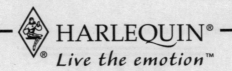

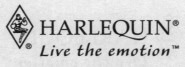

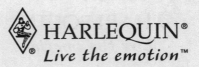

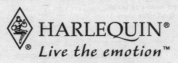

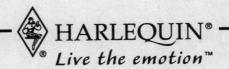